A Snow Day

During my time at primary school I ⸻ re
still my friends to this very day. I h⸺ ⸺ e
was Charlie McCusker. It was the e⸺
the teacher says "it's snowing and I think there is going to ⸺ ⸺ n,
so we are closing the school for three days". So myself and my two
brothers, Con and John, left for home. In the 1950's everyone walked to
school. There were no cars or television and no telephones. The only
telephone was at the post office one mile away. About half way home we
met daddy coming to meet us with big coats. He wrapped a big coat around
me. The coat he wrapped around me was my mother's good coat. I believe
if daddy hadn't come to take us home we would never have made it home
alive. The snow seemed to just get deeper and deeper all the time. The
snow was so deep; I was hardly fit to walk. I was never as glad to see home
in my life. I told my mother I was never going back to school again. I am
seventy years of age now and I still hate to see snow. In the 1950s if you
saw a car any day it was a big deal, and it was always the doctor or the
priest or the police. The roads were rough stones. Only the major roads had
tarmac. Our home was one and a half miles from the school. By the time
we got home, the snow was about nine inches deep. When we got home I
was so tired I cried. My mother gave me a big bowl of chicken soup. After
I drank the soup I fell asleep.

After I woke up, most of the day had gone, so for the rest of the day I did
very little. I tried to read a little, but I could not read because the house was
too dark. There was no electricity and it was too early to light the tilley
lamps and I could not concentrate. From then until bed time, I helped my
mother wash the eggs to have them ready for the egg man to collect on
Thursday morning. I went to bed early and rose early next morning. I had
breakfast and did my chores. My chores consisted of bringing in turf for
the fire, milking a sick cow named Tuffie, gave Tuffie water and fed her
some hay and nuts. Then I mucked out her pen and gave her clean bedding.
Then I left Tuffie and gave the pigs some skimmed milk. It was easy to
give the pigs the milk, because all you had to do was turn on a tap. Once
you turned on the tap, you could not leave it until you turned it off again,
because pigs are gluttons. They would drink until they burst. After that,
myself and my brothers went out sledging in the field across the road. The

field across the road had a very steep hill, so it was perfect for sledging. We played up and down that hill until dark.

Next morning was Friday. I was up and out of bed early and did my chores and got back into the house. The snow was almost gone. If any of you lived in a farm house in the 1950's, you would know how horrible it is during a snow storm, with everybody in and out all the time with wet boots leaving the floor wet. I decided I would go to Charlie's house. Charlie and I were so close that at school we were known as 'The Terrible Twins'. Charlie lived above in Seskinore, about one mile from our house. As I walked up through The Seskinore Planting, the lane was almost clear of snow due to the large trees shading the road. It was beautiful. The trees were covered with snow just like perfect Christmas trees. The large beech trees stood along the sides of the road were mighty. I don't think I ever saw them as big and the bark so shiny. I arrived at Charlie's house. I met Charlie and we played football a little while. Then we went to the river to catch minnows. We could not find any minnows as it was too cold. We went back to the house. Charlie's father worked in Barinscort and would not be home until late, so Charlie had a lot of chores. I helped him do his chores. We fed the cows and carried in the fodder for the cows in the morning. We fed the hens and the ducks and foddered the donkey and closed it in for the night. By this time, it was nearly dark. We watched two Reindeer down the field until Charlie's mum called us in for supper. When we had supper we talked for a while as Charlie's mum and two sisters washed up. I decided it was time to go home. Charlie walked with me to the corner and we stood and talked for a long time until we got cold. I left Charlie and headed for home on my own

It was very cold with a slight breeze blowing. The snow was starting to drop from the trees, as there was a thaw starting to set in. As I walked along the road as I had done a million times before, everything went well until I reached a place called Bets Bray. As I approached the bottom of the hill, I heard footsteps and rattling of chains behind me. I got scared and I started walking faster. The faster I walked the faster the chains came, so I started to run. The chains started to run so I stopped. The chains stopped so I walked. Then the chains walked too. I was so scared, the hair stood on my head as a chill ran down my back. I started to run and the chains started

2

to run. The chains kept coming closer and closer until I could feel them right on my heels. I tripped and fell over. When I fell I hurt my knee and my hands. The chains stopped. I got up and started to run again. I ran so hard and screamed so loud you could have heard me in Fintona. Next, I got a push from behind and I fell again. This time the chains did not stop. I was not fit to run one inch further. As I lay on the road I could feel the chains and claws all over me. I thought aliens had caught me and were tying me up with chains to take me away. All that I knew was, whatever they were, they were not human. I screamed and I screamed. I screamed so loud that Daddy heard me. Daddy and my big brother James came running. Daddy lifted me up as James ran after the chains. The chains turned out to be old Miss McClintock's two old goats, tied one to the other with a big chain. I was lucky that Daddy and Jim were outside and heard me scream. If they hadn't heard me, I would have died of shock and would have been known as the only man who was killed by a goat. I will never walk that road again on my own.

The horse doctor

One morning when I was about ten years old, my father went out to discover he had a sick cow. I was sent to fetch Charlie The horse doctor. I walked the quarter mile up the road to fetch Charlie. On finding Charlie and informing him about the sick cow, Charlie says "I will go down and see the cow immediately". At that, I left for home. Half-way home Charlie passed me on his bicycle. When I arrived home, Daddy was not at home. I heard the hens making a racket. I thought there was a fox at the hens so I went to the hen house. On entering I found Charlie in the process of killing a hen and he already had two hen's dead. On challenging Charlie there was nothing wrong with the hens it was the cow that was sick, Charlie says the cow has a bad chill and he needed the hens to make chicken soup. Myself and Charlie left the hen house with Charlie carrying the three dead hens. Charlie then went to the boiler house and put the hens into the boiler, feathers and all. He filled the boiler with about five gallons of water, put the lid on the boiler and lit it. He then ordered me to make him tea. I went to the kitchen and told my mother Charlie wanted tea. My mother says "tell him to come in". I tell Charlie to come in. He comes in and my mother gives him tea and a sandwich. Charlie eats the sandwich and drinks the tea. He sits and talks to my mother for a long time. He tells my mother he has made soup for the cow and that he was waiting for it to cool. Sometime later, Charlie goes back to the boiler and stirs in a full tin of Colman's mustard and then starts to bottle the chicken soup. He then goes to the byre and puts three full bottles into the cow and watches the cow for a while. He tells me he will come back in the morning and give her three more bottles. He would have to come every day until the cow had drank all the soup and by that time she should be better. At that he left for home

When daddy arrived home he wasn't too pleased about the hens. He said to me "when he comes tomorrow, whatever you do, don't let him near the hens". Next morning, about ten o'clock, Charlie arrives and gives the cow another three bottles of the soup and leaves again. Next day Charlie arrives and goes into the byre. Daddy arrives into the byre just as Charlie was giving the cow the third bottle of soup. Daddy asks Charlie what was wrong with the cow. Charlie says "the cow has a chill and I am giving her chicken soup and mustard to warm her up". Daddy says "give her no more of that stuff. The vet will be coming in a short while to examiner her".

Charlie says "the vet will know no more than me". Charlie had one daughter named Sally who was married and living in Australia. Charlie started telling stories about how good a vet he was. One he told was that when his daughter Sally was a teenager, she became very sick and the doctor sent her to the hospital. After two weeks in hospital she was sent home to die they could do nothing for her. "As a last resort I examined her myself and discovered her kidneys were completely done. So, after diagnosis I gave her a kidney transplant using a sheep's kidney and it was completely successful". Daddy laughed and said "I might have to get the vet to give the cow a kidney transplant and he could use a hen's kidney!" The vet arrived and diagnosed the cow with a blockage and there was nothing he could do. One thing you can say about the horse doctor, we lost three good chickens but the cow died with a warm belly.

John McGinn and Billy Kane

When I first met John McGinn, I was a child and John was a full grown man. John came to work for my father on the farm. John and I hit it off right away. He was a very big man, standing six feet three inches tall, with broad shoulders. John had the mental age of a twelve-year-old. I know very little about John's background other than what he told me. He was born in the Townland of Brackey in the Parish of Beragh. When I knew John he was married and lived outside Seskinore. John and his wife had no family. John was a hard worker and loved animals. He loved horses and was one of the best at working with horses. It was said that John was one of the best ploughmen in all Ireland.

John would take me with him out to the fields. I would sit on the horses back or sit in the cart, while John would walk and lead the horse. When we got to the field John would start working I would walk back to the house. As time moved on I grew up and moved on. John moved on as well. When tractors took over John kept a horse. He kept a working horse until the day he died. I married and got on with my life. Now and again our paths would have crossed. When we met we could always have a good conversation. The conversation would always be about horses and ploughing. On talking to John, he would always make it clear I was special to him and that I was his best friend. He would tell me things that he would not tell anyone else about himself or his wife, mostly about disagreements with his wife.

One day I was out for a walk and John came down the road on his bicycle he stops and says "I was on my way down to your house to see you". John never came to my house ever, so I knew this was serious right away. John told me a story I found hard to believe, but it was true. He says "did you hear my wife died and the trouble I got into?" I said "I am sorry, I never heard. When did she die?" John says "she died two weeks ago and she was buried yesterday". He said "very few people know, because I told nobody and the police were out with me". I said "what were the police out for?" He said "my wife got sick, and she said she was dying and she wanted the priest. I took out my bicycle and went down to the post office to ring for a priest. I asked the Postmaster to ring for a priest as I did not know how to use a phone. The Postmaster snapped the head of me and says "there's the phone and ring your priest yourself". When I came home she was dead. I cried and never told anyone for a week. Then I told a neighbour and he told the police. The police sorted everything out". I said "what do you want me to do?" He said "I want you to promise that when I am dying you will get me a priest". I said "I will". John says "promise?" and I said "I promise". I passed this promise over and thought nothing more about it. Then the conversation turned to ploughing and horses. From that day on every time I met John, he told me the story of his wife's death and always finished with the words, "when I am dying you will get the priest for me?" I would answer "I will, John". Then it was "promise me?" "I promise you John" and that would be the end of that conversation until the next time we met. Ten to twelve years passed and this conversation took place on several occasions.

I hadn't seen or heard anything about John for about two or three years and then one day, somebody told me John was sick. It never bothered me. Then I heard he was in the hospital and was back out again. I passed no remarks because I had enough going on in my life without worrying about an old man like John, and I soon forgot about him. About six or seven weeks later, I went to bed as usual and said my prayers and went to sleep. I had a dream. I dreamt I was in the Isle of Man on holiday and a knock came to my door. I opened the door and an old neighbour man by the name of Billy Kane was standing at the door. Billy was a man who had no home. He was an ex-soldier and he worked for farmers around the country. Every farmer Billy worked for had to supply him with three square meals a day, six days a week and at night Billy slept anywhere he could get his head down. Usually some farmers shed. By this time Billy was about ninety years of age and had been living in a nursing home for about ten or fifteen years. Beside Billy stood a priest by the name of Father Michael Doherty, who had been a Curate in our parish some years earlier. I had not seen him in years. As I stood at the door, Billy stood in front of me and says "Bridie is dead". Bridie was my sister. Billy and Father Doherty would slide back from me by about twenty feet and would come forward again and Billy would say "Bridie is dead". This happened repeatedly at least twenty times until I woke up. When I woke I was crying. I woke my wife and told her about my dream. She says maybe Billy is dead. I got up and dressed and rang the nursing home to enquire about Billy. The home said Billy was well and was up washing for breakfast.

By this time my wife was up and had made tea and toast. We talked about the dream as we drank our tea and did not know what to make of it. Then it dawned on me that Uncle Jim had been sick, so I decided I would call round and see him. Jim lived alone, about a mile away. Jim would be wondering why I called so early in the morning. I was to cut turf for Jim so I decided that if he wasn't sick I would tell him I was going to his turf on Saturday. I drove round to Jim's house. When I arrived, I met Jim coming from the well with a bucket of water. I talked to Jim for a short while told him I would see him on Saturday. I left Jim and headed for home. As I drove up the road, I drove past John's house. As I drove, I noticed John's door open and I thought "was John alright?" I stopped and got out of the car. I walked over to John's open door and shouted "are you in John?" I heard a sound from the room that I knew wasn't right. I walked in through the open door. The first door to my left was John's bedroom. Through the open bedroom door I saw John sitting on the side of his bed. Between his legs he had a bucket and he was continually being sick into the bucket. I entered the room to ask John did he want a doctor. He said he did and he wanted some groceries from the shop. He told me the three or four items he wanted. I told him I would get him the groceries and phone the doctor.

I left him at that. It was coming near time for me to go to work and the shop didn't open until nine o'clock, so I went down to my brother John's house I told him about John McGinn being sick and needing the doctor and the groceries and asked would he get them as I had to go to work. He says "I will ring the doctor and will get him the groceries as soon as I finish milking the cows". At that, I left him and went to my work and forgot about John. When I arrived home from work and had my dinner I decided I would go round and see John. When I arrived I went into the house and there it was the same as I left it in the morning, with John sitting on the side of the bed still being sick. I said "did you see the doctor?" He said "he was here this morning and he wanted me to go to hospital and I did not want to go". I said "why did you not go? You're not well!" He said "I was in the hospital and I signed myself out because one of the nurses was very cheeky towards me". I said "well you need to go now because you can't stay here". He said "No, I am going near no hospital".

So I left him and went home. When I arrived home, I told my wife about John. She says "I will go around and see him". My wife is a qualified and experienced SRN (Registered General Nurse).

My wife and myself drive round to John's house. We see the door still open and John still sitting on the side of the bed being sick. She tries to persuade John to go to hospital with no success. As I drove my wife home, she says "you may stay with John tonight because he is very ill". So I dropped my wife home and went back to John's house. I tried again to talk him into going to the hospital. He still refused, until about one am when he says "I will go to the hospital if I get into Bridie's ward". My sister Bridie was a sister in ward twelve. I said "I will go and arrange it". So I left and went down to my brother Con's house which was nearest, and he had a phone. I woke up Con and told him my story, and that I wanted to use his phone. I phoned Bridie and she wasn't a bit pleased. She said "bring him on in and I will phone and explain, and the staff will be waiting for you". So I drive back up to Jim's house and tell him that the arrangements are made for him to go to Bridies ward, and I was to bring him in straight away. But John being John says "No, I will only go in if Bridie brings me iin". So I had to go back down and rise Con out of bed again to use his phone. I phoned Bridie and she wasn't a bit pleased. She says "it's after two am and I must go to work in the morning!" I explained to her how sick John was and I had to go to work in the morning too. Bridie says "alright, I will go down now and see him". My brother Conn says "I will go with you myself", and my brother drives back up to John's house. Ten minutes later Bridie arrives like a bear with a sore head. She goes into the room to John and feels his pulse. At that, she calms down and says "the sooner we get him to the hospital the better", so we arm John out and put him into the front seat of the car. Myself and Con get into the back and Bridie drives. The car had no sooner moved when John fell asleep. Bridie reached over and felt his pulse, nobody spoke, and I was sure he was dead. Ten minutes later we arrived at the hospital. There the doctor and nurses were waiting and took over.

I decided I would go to the vending machine while Bridie talked to a nurse in the office. On my way to the vending machine I remembered John's story and the priest. So I went to a nurse and asked her to phone for a priest for John. She said she would. About fifteen minutes later, the priest arrived and went in to see John. When the priest came out from John, he spoke to us for five or ten minutes and went on his way. At that, we decided it was time to go home. Before I went home I went into see John. John was sitting up in the bed with a smile from ear to ear, a completely new man. I say to him, "the priest was in with you?" John says "aye, and he anointed me". Then he says "Mickey, when I get out of here, I will not forget you for bringing me in here tonight". That was John's last words. Within minutes he was dead.

Billy Kane was the man who came to me in the dream. I will now tell you the story of Billy. Billy was a very strange man. I knew him very well. Billy was an ex-soldier. He claimed he was in the army during the Second World War. He had a brother named Jamie, who I met a few times, but I did not know him. Billy was nicked named 'The Gunner', but you dare not let him hear you call him it. Once when I was about nine or ten years old, I called Billy 'The Gunner' and he nearly killed me. Only my father came along in time, Billy would have me choked to death. Billy had no home; he worked for farmers all around the country. He worked from day light until dark, six days a week. Billy's wages were one pound per day, plus three meals to his liking. At night time, Billy slept anywhere he could get his head down - usually behind a ditch or in some farmers hay.

Billy was a very tall man, with a full head of snow white hair and he was the fastest walker I ever knew. Every day, seven days a week, winter or summer, Billy would go to the river and wash and shave in the cold water. In all the years I knew Billy, I never once saw him unshaved or wearing dirty clothes. It was believed that Billy's father and mother died when Billy and Jamie were very young, and that Billy and Jamie reared themselves. It is believed that they walked the roads by day, and at night they would go into the fields and milk cows and drink the milk. That was how they survived. They were seen on several occasions, one holding a cow and the other milking.

Every Saturday night when Billy received his wages, he would go to the house of an old man who lived on his own by the name of Jack Stars. He would wait for Kelly's mobile groceries' van to come. Kelly's mobile van came about ten o'clock every Saturday night. When the van arrived, Billy would go to the van and buy one pound of sausages, one pound of bacon, one loaf of bread and one-half pound of butter. He then goes up into Jack's house to fry the bacon and sausages in the butter. Then Jack and himself would eat the whole thing. This was their weekly treat. Jack's treat was the bacon and sausages. Billy's treat was that he could sleep on Jack's floor for one night.

On Sunday morning, when Billy rose, he went as usual to the river and washed. He would then go to ten thirty mass in Seskinore. When the collection plate came around, Billy would put the remainder of his wages on the plate. So that meant that Billy worked all week for one pound of bacon, one pound of bacon and one loaf of bread. On one occasion Billy threw a five-pound note and some change onto the plate. The priest lifted the five pound note and handed it back to Billy, saying "you need that more than me". Billy refused to take back the five pounds and kicked up that big a fuss that the priest had to take the fiver.

Billy became sick and had to go in to hospital. After a week he was released from hospital. Next day Billy arrived into our house, about eight in the morning. My mother gave him a breakfast. He told her he had been in hospital. My mother asked him where he slept last night. He says "I slept in Baxter's hay". My mother says "Billy, you cannot be lying out at night and you sick!" Billy says "what else am I going to do? I have nowhere to live". My mother says "you will have to go to a home". Billy says "I am so sick I would go anywhere to rest my head". My mother gave me a phone number and sent me to the post office and instructed me to phone the authorities and ask for a Mr Vance. I was to explain about Billy, that he was sick and that he had nowhere to live. I took out my bicycle and cycled one mile to the post office. Out in the yard at the post office was the telephone box. I phoned the number my mother my mother gave me and told the operator what I wanted. She put through to the authorities. I spoke to Mr Vance and explained my case. He asked me for all the details and I told him all I knew. He says "I will come out immediately and see him. Tell him to stay at your house until I get there". On arriving home, I told my mother that Mr Vance was coming out to see Billy and he was to wait until he came. She said that was lovely.

A short time later, Mr Vance arrived. He took Billy down to the room and interviewed him. After a period of time he came back to the kitchen, and told my mother he had to go back to the office to make arrangements. He wanted Billy to stay here until he came back. My mother says "I have no way of keeping him tonight". Mr Vance assured her that he would have some where for Billy before night. My mother says "that's all right". At that, Mr Vance left. He arrived back later that day and interviewed Billy again. This coming and going and interviews went on all day. I assume Mr Vance was doing interviews and was going back to his office to make phone calls. That day my mother made Billy his dinner and looked after him all day while Mr Vance came and went. Mr Vance worked very hard on Billy's case all day. Late on in the evening, Mr Vance told my mother and father that Billy did not know when he was born or what age he was. During his interview with Billy and asking about things he remembered, he calculated that Billy was over eighty years of age and would qualify for a pension. He had found Billy a place in a government nursing home in Strabane some thirty miles away. My father says "that's very far away, Billy wouldn't know where Strabane is or would not even have been near Strabane in his life!" Mr Vance says "it's the only place with a spare bed I can find, and Billy has agreed to go. I will get him transferred as soon as a vacancy turns up nearer here". At that, Billy gets into Mr Vance's car and Mr Vance and Billy head of for Strabane.

The Following Sunday, my father, mother and I, drove down to Strabane to visit Billy and bring him some sundries and see how he was. Billy was content and thankful for having a bed. Some weeks later, Billy was transferred to a home in Clogher, which was only about ten miles from where we lived. Billy got to know a local farmer who he did bits of work for. He was happy and on top of the world. Every so often, my father and mother would visit Billy. One evening Billy arrived at our house. He informed my father that he had walked out of the home and walked the eight miles from the home to our house. His reason for leaving was that he had no clothes, and that when he asked for a suit, the Matron informed him that he was getting no suit, as he wanted the suit for going to mass on a Sunday. She said if he stopped going to mass she would get him all the clothes he needed. Billy refused point blank to go back to the home. Daddy tried everything to persuade Billy, but he refused. And Mr Vance could not be contacted. Daddy contacted the Parish Priest who arrived and informed Billy that he would get him all the clothes he needed so Billy agreed to my father taking him back to the home. Next day, St. Vincent De Paul visited Billy and got him clothes. It is my understanding that as it was a Government home the Matron was suspended. From that day until the day Billy died, St. Vincent De Paul visited Billy every month and got Billy anything he needed. He would not wear anything belonging to the home.

Billy lived for a long number of years thereafter in the home. It was in the late eighties or early ninety's when one morning, a Priest by the name of Fr Carrigan approached me at work and informed me Billy was dead. He asked me did I know of any relations of Billy. I informed him that Billy had no relations, that he had one brother named Jamie and that he was dead years ago and that Jamie was buried in the Dublin Road Cemetery. He took my information on board only to arrive back a couple of hours later, and inform me that the council had went through every record they had, and could not find any record of a grave belonging to a Jamie Kane. He also said that nobody he asked knew anything about Jamie or for that matter about Billy, and he wanted to know if I could give him any more information. All I could tell him was that the grave was on the sloped ground facing towards the Golf links. I told him to contact Jack McGinn, that he was the undertaker and that Jamie had worked for Jack's uncle. Jack McGinn was a very old man and a retired undertaker who was suffering from Alzheimer's and hadn't been out of the house for years.

Fr Carrigan went to visit Jack and Fr Carrigan nor could Jack's family believe what they were hearing about Billy and Jamie. When Fr Carrigan named Billy and Jamie, Jack remembered everything about them. He told him that he would never find a grave in the name Jamie Kane because it was in the name of Jack McGinn as he had bought the grave and buried Jamie because he had died penniless.   He also told him the whole history of Billy and Jamie growing up in starvation and having no parents or house. Jack told Fr Carrigan about them lying out under ditches and sheds all their lives. He also told him the story of Billy and the money and the priest. I will never forget Billy's face when I bought him the first choc ice he had ever seen or tasted. I also introduced him to his first ever safety razor.

Fr Carrigan came back to me and asked would I get some men to carry Billy's coffin. I said I would. I arranged for myself, my brother Dominic and two neighbours Stephen McCabe and James Breen to carry the coffin. Next morning as arranged, the funeral took place. Myself, Dominic, Stephen, James and my cousin and two staff from the home were the only people in the church who had ever known Billy. There about one hundred people in the church for the normal morning mass. None would have known Billy or even ever heard tell of Billy until that day. Fr Carrigan said the mass and the funeral service. During his Eulogy, he told the congregation about this man Billy Kane who we were burying that day. He told them about him never having a home, and how he gave his money to the Church every Sunday morning. He told them about the man with Alzheimer's disease who was fit to remember Billy and remember where his brother Jamies grave was. It was ironic that when Billy died, he was brought to the morgue in Omagh hospital where he was laid out beside the Duke of Abercorn, who had died at around the same time as Billy. The Duke owned thousands of acres of land and was the richest man in the County of Tyrone. We carried the coffin from the church to the hearse. Not one person left the church before the coffin, and the entire congregation walked behind the hearse to the bottom of the street. Fr Carrigan gave Billy the nicest send-off I ever heard.

Johnny Dooley

During the 1950's the town of Omagh where I lived was full of men with lost limbs. I was young and I wondered why our town had so many men with only one leg or only one arm. Johnny Dooley was one of these men who had only one leg. I became good friends with Johnny and he explained to me that all these men lost their limbs during the Second World War. Johnny would stand at the bottom of Main Street with a handcart selling fruit. On Thursdays and Fridays he would be selling fish. You could hear Johnny all over town, shouting, "Ally Cally-fornia American apples for sale! two dimes each!". In today's money two dimes would equal about one sixth of five pence. Johnny had a very close friend by the name of Charlie Wilson. Johnny and Charlie knew every trick in the book.

One nice Tuesday morning, Johnny was selling his 'Ally Cally-fornia American Apples' when three American soldiers came down the street, named Mark, Jack and Georgie. The soldiers stopped with Johnny and bought some apples. Johnny and the soldiers got talking about the war. Johnny told them he was a British soldier and how he had lost his leg at the front. The conversation continued about different solders - German, French, Australian, American and British. Until one of the American soldiers says to Johnny, "do you ever see any IRA men around here?" Johnny says, "there's one comes walking up the street every day". Georgie says "will you show him to us? We would love to see an IRA man". Johnny says, "I could, but I am a British soldier and it could be dangerous, so I would have to get paid for taking the risk". Mark says, "how much would it cost?". Johnny says, "one shilling for each man". The soldiers agreed to come back to Johnny's stall at twelve o clock the next day to pay Johnny one shilling each and Johnny would show them an IRA man.

The American soldiers bought some more apples and went on their way. That night Johnny meets up with his friend Charlie Wilson and tells Charlie about the Americans. Next day Johnny arrives at the bottom of Main Street with his handcart and apples. He starts selling his apples as usual. Sometime later, nine American soldiers arrive and give Johnny one shilling each. The soldiers bought apples and waited and waited. They bought more apples and waited some more. After a period, Charlie Wilson comes around the corner of Townsville Street, speaks to Johnny and walks up Mainstreet. Charlie was wearing a pair of knee length boots, a pair of riding breeches a black three-quarter length coat, carrying a blackthorn stick. Johnny says "there's an IRA man". Now the nine American soldiers walk up the street after Charlie. Charlie turns across Church Street on to Courthouse Street and then turns right on to Bridge Street and back onto Main Street, nine American soldiers still following him. Half way down Main Street Charlie turns to the soldiers and shouts at them, "what are you following me for"? Charlie makes a run for the soldiers waving his stick in the air. The soldiers run down Main Street with Charlie running after them as they run past Johnnie Dooley Johnny laughs and shouts, "The IRA runs American Marines out of town!"

I will tell you another of Johnny's tricks. There was a large British Army Garrison station in our town. Every time a new regiment came to town, they brought with them many recruiting officers. The recruiting officers would parade around the town looking for new recruits. When they signed up a recruit, they would give him one shilling. In today's money that would be five pence. Johnny Dooley would go to the local restaurant and sit behind a table while Charlie Wilson would find a recruiting officer and tell him there were a man in the restaurant who wanted to join the army. Charlie would bring the officer to the restaurant and set him down in front of Johnny. The officer would interview Johnny and sign him up. When the paper work was completed, the officer would give Johnny one shilling. When Johnny received the shilling, he would stand up lift his crutch and say, "well I will go now". The officer would have to pay Charlie another shilling to stay where he was, as he could not be seen to have recruited a man with one leg. Johnny would sit down, while Charlie would go to look for the next officer, to complete the same procedure. Johnny Dooley and Charlie Wilson would collect two shillings from every recruiting officer in town. One officer would not tell another that he had signed a recruit into the army with one leg.

Now, Charlie Wilson worked for a local farmer the name of Mr Ford. Charlie loved a few drinks on weekends and was in the habit of being late for work on a Monday morning. One Monday morning Charlie turned in late as usual. Mr Ford confronted Charlie about being late. Charlie never spoke until early that evening. Charlie picked up his coat and headed for home. Mr Ford asks "where are you going, it's not near quitting time yet". Charlie says "I know, but I must go, because I was late this morning and its bad luck to have two lates in one day".

On another Monday at Halloween time Charlie did not turn in for work. On Tuesday morning Mr Ford confronts Charlie, "where were you yesterday?" Charlie says, "Mr Ford if you had the dream I had on Sunday night you would not be out yesterday, today, or tomorrow". Mr Ford says, "what was your dream?" Charlie says, "I dreamed I had died and I was in hell. I was sitting down at the back of the room and I was freezing with cold. Up beside the fire was a big armchair. I made my way up to the armchair, and just as I was sitting down, the big devil hit me a blow and knocked me down to the back of the room. This happened several times during the night. Eventually I lost my temper and I asked the big devil why he wouldn't let me sit in the chair beside the fire and he said, I can't let you sit in that chair, because I am saving that chair for a very important person, by the name of Mr Ford".

Lost Love

It was the year of 1969 and the troubles in Northern Ireland were just starting to heat up. James Mc Williams was living at home with his mother Mary on a farm. James was an only son. His father had died in a farm accident when James was fourteen. James and his father were very close. When he died James was devastated. James was now twenty-one years of age and he was living the happy-go-lucky life. He had a good job, he worked hard, earned good money and drove a nice car and played hard. James worked as an engineer with Road Services. As his father was dead and there was only James and his mother James helped her out as much as he could on the small farm. His neighbour Daniel Kelly was his best friend from the day they started primary school they saw each other every day and did everything together. They both sat in the same class in primary school and then in the same class in secondary school. They went to the same university. Both qualified as engineers and James got himself a job with Road Services and Daniel got himself a job with a construction company.

On a lovely Friday evening shortly before the Twelfth of July, James' friend Daniel and James decided they would go down to Knock Moyle hall and play table tennis which they did on a regular basis. They travelled down to Knock Moyle and discovered that they were too early, the hall wasn't open. They waited for a short period of time but no one came to open the hall. They then decided to go back to Omagh and go to the cinema and watch a film. When they arrived back in Omagh, the town was filling up with people and they had trouble finding a parking spot. They found a parking spot in a car park behind the cinema. As James parked the car, two nice girls walked past and Daniel opened the car door and shouts to the girls to wait for him. The girls stop and wait. James gets out of the car and locks it and by this time Daniel is standing talking and laughing with the girls. James joins them. They walked along with the girls up the alley way which leads from the car park to Main Street. As they get talking, James being the man that he is, found out their names and where they were going. They were two protestant girls going to an Orange parade in the town and their names were Marlene Wilson and Janet Johnston. They were both friends and they were from a town fifteen miles away. They walked with the girls up the alleyway to Main Street and when they reached Main Street they said goodbye to the girls. The girls turned right up Market Street and the boys turned left towards the cinema and went on about their business.

As they enter the cinema and take their seats, Daniel says to James "I am going to marry that Janet she is lovely" and James laughs. They are just in time for the start of the film. During the film James noticed Daniel was very restless and never stopped moving about. He asked him several times what was wrong with him and he said nothing. The film wasn't very good. About half-way through the film, Daniel says "I am leaving this is rubbish". James says "stay another while, it's not that bad". Daniel was still very agitated. After about another ten minutes Daniel stands up and says "I am going" and heads for the door. James follows him and they leave the cinema. They walk out of the cinema on to Market Street. The Orange parade had just passed and the street was full of Orange men with bowler hats and bands men. There standing across the street was Marlene and Janet, Daniel's face lights up when he sees them. He shouts over to them and they come over and join Daniel and James. James gets talking to Marlene while Daniel talks to Janet. Marlene smiles and says "call me Marlene that's what my friends call me". James says "it's nice to know that I am your friend", Marlene laughs. Marlene and James get on well together and they enjoy each other's company. James thinks Marlene has the most beautiful smile when she laughs and he tells her so. Marlene and Janet are at university studying to become primary school teachers. They are both in their second year. Marlene says "look where Daniel and Janet are". Daniel and Janet were standing down the street about thirty meters away holding hands and watching an accordion band play.

Marlene tells James that her and Janet were staunch loyalist and that her father was a police man. James said it didn't make much difference to him what religion she was other than he did not like police. Marlene said it made no difference to her either, but it would make a difference to Janet, her father would go stone mad even at the thought of Janet holding hands with a catholic. James says "leave them to it they will be alright". Daniel is never backward when it comes to girls. Marlene says "no, come on down and join them". James takes her hand as they walk down and join Daniel and Janet. Marlene says something to Janet about the boys being Catholics and they both laughed, James didn't pick up what she said nor didn't care.

Daniel says "Janet and Marlene are going to a young farmers dance and I am going with them", Marlene asks James "will you come?" James says "why not". Janet looks at her watch and says "it's too early to go to the dance yet, what will we do until then?" Daniel says "we will go someplace for something to eat, I'm starving". James says "that's the best news I have heard today as my stomach thinks my throats cut". The girls laugh, and Janet says "I never heard that one before". Daniel asks the girls would they like to join them for something to eat. They both say yes. The four of them walk up the street to a cafe. They take their seats in the café and order four fish and chips and four glasses of milk. They enjoy the fish and chips, and the girls seem to enjoy theirs. James and Daniel pay for the meals. As they were eating their meal, James looked across the table at Marlene and Janet eating and talking ninety to the dozen. He thinks to himself that with her brown hair and blue eyes, Marlene was the nicest looking woman he had ever seen in his entire life.

They finish their meals, leave the café and walk down the street. As they walk down the street they meet three orange men whom Janet and Marlene know by name. The girls stop to talk to them and the boys walk on to the entrance of the alleyway, which leads to the car park where James car was parked. There the boys waited for the girls. When the girls joined them again, Janet says "that was my brother William and his friends. They wanted to know who you were". James asked "did you tell them" Janet said "no you must be joking thinking we would tell them we were with two Catholics!" There were still a lot of people walking about the street.

The four of them walked down the alleyway to where the car is parked. Daniel gets into the front of the car beside James, and the girls get into the back. James drives about three miles to the dance hall. They talk and laugh a lot. It was only when they arrived at the hall they discover it's an Orange hall. They had some good laughs on the way. James did not want to go into an Orange hall because he thought it too dangerous, and he was afraid. Daniel and Janet reassured him it would be all right as it was a

Farmers Union dance and they would think they were farmers. Marlene laughs and says "are you afraid I will shoot you?" James says "No, but your father might".

Daniel, the two girls and James paid the entrance fee and enter the hall. The hall was decorated in union flags they moved up the right-hand side of the hall and sat down. There were only thirty or forty people in the hall and it seemed they were all looking at James and Daniel as if they had two heads each. The band started to play and people started to dance, as the hall began to fill up with people. Janet and Marlene danced every dance and were really enjoying themselves, but Daniel and James did not dance as they felt uncomfortable and out of place being there. Every now and again Janet and Marlene would come back to talk to them. They would then go off to dance again.

After a period, Marlene came over to them and told Daniel and James that they would be better to leave as someone had recognised them and knew that they were Catholics. Marlene said that her and Janet could not be seen continuing to talk to them. The boys got up to their feet and headed for the door, as they went there seemed to be a crowd gathering around the door. Daniel was in front and James was right behind him. Daniel was pushed and staggered down the step. He ignored it and walked on followed by James. They quickened their pace, as they knew that five or six men were following them. By the time they made it to the car, they were running with the men running after them and trying to hit them. They were shouting at them "go home you fenian b_____s" among other things. The men were running so close behind them they could not get into the car, so they ran past the car and up the road until they came to a gate into a field. James and Daniel jumped the gate into the field and as it was dark the men did not see where they went. James and Daniel ran up the field. The men stopped at the gate. James and Daniel waited up the field until they thought the men had left. They slipped down the field as quietly as they could in the dark and climbed over the gate. As they reached the car a crowd of people came running out of the hall. They jumped into the car and took off with the crowd shouting and banging on the roof of James car. James recognised a woman who banged the windscreen of his car and cracked it. After they got clear of the crowd, James says to Daniel "it will be awhile before we go back there again". James could not believe it when Daniel says "I have arranged to meet Janet again". James says "Daniel, are you stupid? It was Janet who told the Orange men we were Catholics and set us for a beating!" Daniel says "it doesn't matter what she done, I am going to marry her". James laughs and says "that will be the day".

James drops Daniel home and then drives the half mile to his own home. Morning came and James forgets all about the whole affair. About two weeks later, Daniel came to James and informs him he has been in contact with Janet and that he had arranged to go to see her. He wanted James to come with him as he did not want go alone. He had arranged to meet her at Marlene's house because Janet was afraid of her family finding out she was going out with a catholic. Daniel said that Marlene also wanted to see James. Daniel says "I am going up to see Janet tonight and that I want you to come". James says "I will not be going near any RUC man's house", Daniel says "you must come because if you don't come I will not be able to go and see Janet". James says "If you go up there you are looking for trouble, it will be worse than the Orange hall". Daniel says "no don't be silly I was up there a couple times, and nobody bothered me". James thought for a moment and says to himself it might be worth going to see Marlene again. So to please Daniel and with the chance of speaking to Marlene, James decides to go with him. He tells Daniel "I will not be getting out of the car as I would never trust a RUC man". Daniel laughed. It was easy for Daniel because he was never afraid of anyone or anything. That evening Danial picks up James and they drive up to Marlene's house. It was a nice three-bedroom bungalow with lovely lawn and garden.

No sooner had Daniel the car parked when Marline comes out and invites them to come into the house. James had no choice but to go into the house because Marlene was so nice, and he could not refuse her. James gets out of the car and stands looking at the breath taking scenery down over the Clogher valley. James walks to the door stands for a moment wondering whether to go in or turn back. Marlene and Daniel had already gone into the house. Marlene's mother Margaret came to the door and says "come on in". James went into the house and Margaret made him feel welcome. When James saw Marlene's mother it was easy to know where Marlene got her smile from. Margaret showed him into the sitting room and told him to take a seat. James sat down as Margaret left the room. Sitting there on his own he looked around the room. It was a nice room with a brown and green carpet with matching curtains, a matching three piece suite with a side board sitting under the window. On top of the sideboard in the living room was an RUC man's cap with that hated red and green symbol of the crown and harp. James ignored it. As he sat there he could hear Daniel and Marlene talking in the kitchen but he could not hear what they were saying. He thought to himself "what I am doing here" and was about to get up and leave when he heard a car come into the driveway. He looked out of the window and saw Janet park her car and get out. He watched as Daniel left the house and joined Janet. They talked a moment got into Daniel's car and drove off down the drive. James wondered what he was going to do as he was sitting in an RUC man's house with no car. He felt more comfortable when Marlene came into the room and started to talk to him .

Marlene's mother made James and Marlene nice tea and joined them in the sitting room. The three of them talked a lot and got on well together. They talked about the Orange hall and Marlene's mother said we could have got a bad beating and that the girls should not have taken us near the place. Margaret said that if James told the police and gave them the name of the woman who broke his windscreen she would be charged and would have to pay to fix the windscreen. She said "it would serve her right and she would think twice next time". Then James nearly went through the floor when Marlene said he did not like the police. Margaret says "don't worry about it, I know a lot of Catholics do not like the police because of instances down through the years". James drank the tea and ate the scones and they talked a long time in each other's company. James said "it is time for me to go home, I would need to phone for someone to come and collect me because I don't think Daniel is coming back tonight". Marlene says "it's all right, I will drive you home when you are ready" James says "I am ready now". Marlene gets the keys for the car and puts on her coat and heads for the door. James says good bye to her mother and thanks her for the tea and follows Marlene out through the door and gets into the passenger seat of the car.

As they drive down the road Marlene talks a lot about everything. Marlene tells James that her mother likes him, James says "I couldn't care less if she liked me or not". He was annoyed because Daniel had drove him to Marlene's house and left him there to get home whatever way he liked and now he realises that it was a conspiracy to get Marlene and him together. They arrived at James house. James wasn't saying too much and was thinking a lot. Marlene was still talking when she stopped the car in front of the house. When she realised that James wasn't in good form she went quiet they sat there in silence for a short period. Not knowing what to say while reaching for the door handle James broke the silence by saying "I would need to go" as he moved to open the door Marline reaches over and catches his hand and says "what's wrong?" James says nothing. Marlene says "is it me?" James says "no", then Marlene says "I know it's because I am a protestant". James couldn't let her go away thinking that because her religion had never crossed his mind. He told her it was Daniel setting him up. Marlene says "don't blame Daniel. It was me, I wanted to see you again". By this time, she was looking straight into his eyes and James could see in her lovely blue eyes that she meant what she said as he looked at her in the light streaming from the window of the house. He thought for a moment "what do I say now" but he didn't have to say a word, it all just happened. He looked at her with a lump in his throat and a flutter in his stomach. He bent over and kissed her on the lips and she just melted into his arms. They kissed and cuddled for a long while and the sun was starting to rise from behind the mountain. Marlene says I would need to go home as I was never in my whole life been out until sun rise.   James opened the car door and gave her a good night kiss. He got out of the car and closed the car door and watched Marlene turn the car and drive into the sun rise. He waved good bye and watched until the car drove out of sight. He walked in a quick pace to the door of the house. He took the door key from his pocket, unlocked the door and gently opened it. He entered the house and closed the door and locked it again. He tiptoed up the stairs, missing the third step from the top as it always squeaked when someone stepped on it. He entered his bed room and went straight to bed as quietly as he could because he didn't want to wake his mother.

James didn't sleep much as there was so much material running through his head. Luckily he wasn't working next day because he didn't sleep until it was time to get up, so he slept in. He woke up at ten past eleven. He jumped out of bed, ran to the bath room and washed his face and had a shave. It was then that he remembered he had the day off. He then relaxed and had nice shower, dressed and went to the kitchen. His mother had just made a pot of nice chicken soup. As he walked into the kitchen his mother set two bowls of soup on the table and sat down. James sat down beside her. Mary says "how did you get home last night, you came in very late?" Making excuses for being late, he said "Daniel dropped me off and something must have happened because he never came back to pick me up. I waited half the night and then a nice girl, a friend of Daniel's girlfriend left me home". After having the soup he walked to the local shop and bought the daily paper. He walked to the bookies and put five pounds on a horse that was running at three o'clock. He walked home and watched the horse racing and lost his five pounds. He read the paper and all this time he can't get Marlene out of his mind. Mary gives him a cup of tea and asks him "what is wrong with you today? You're like someone in love!" It was just then that he realised he was falling in love with Marlene.

Evening came, and James could not wait to see Marlene. When he dresses up and gets ready to go to see Marlene, Mary says "I never saw you dressed as well since your father died, you are like a man in love". It was times like this he wished his father was alive so as he could talk to him and tell him about Marlene. As he was about to leave the house, Mary laughs and says "when am I going to meet her, and what's her name?" James says "you will have to wait because I only have met her myself, and her name is Marlene". Mary says "that's a protestant name". James says "that's right" and walks out through the door not giving her a chance to say something she might regret.

He leaves the house and drives the fifteen miles to Marlene's house. Marlene was not ready and her mother Margaret invited him to come in for a cup of tea. When Margaret showed him into the sitting room, Marlene's father Robert was siting watching television. Margaret introduced James to him as Marlene's friend. He looked at James and mumbled something. James did not pick up on what he said. James sat down and felt uncomfortable because he recognised him and had met him on several checkpoints and had experienced his anti-Catholic bigotry when he was with his friends with their reserve RUC uniform on and carrying their machine guns. Robert wouldn't have been the sharpest knife in the drawer, he only got into the police because he was a top Orange man and had moved from the B. Specials. James knew Robert didn't want him in the house because he was a catholic. James wasn't going to say anything to annoy him because he loved Marlene. Robert says to James "you got into some trouble at the Orange hall? James says "it wasn't too bad". Robert says "it could have been a lot worse and it would have served you right for being there". James said nothing and thought typical RUC, thinking Catholics have no right to be anywhere.

Margaret came in to the living room carrying a tray with tea and biscuits for Robert, James and herself. James sipped the tea and relaxed. !t was easy to relax with Margaret because she talked a lot, but it was not so easy to relax with Robert. Marlene walks into the room and said "I am ready". Her beauty just took the breath from James. Margaret says "Marlene you look beautiful". James stands up and says "I agree with Margaret". Robert just looked over in the direction of Marlene and smiled as much as to say I agree. Margaret gives Marlene a cuddle and says "have a good night". James thanks Margaret for the tea as he and Marlene leave the house. They drive into Enniskillen to have a meal in a hotel as arranged and go to a show in the local theatre. After they left the house Marlene asked James how well he got on with Robert. James says "not very well. He doesn't like me, I tried to speak to him he completely ignored me". Marlene says "don't worry he can be like that at times, especially when it concerns me". James says "I don't care if he speaks to me or not as long as he is not wearing that uniform".

They enter the hotel and the waiter shows them to a table and gives them the menu. Marline asks for a glass of water and James says "I will have the same". Marlene says "I am glad you didn't ask for something stronger when you are driving me" James says "I don't drink". She says "what a coincidence, I don't drink either". She told him that Janet doesn't drink either, and James says "Daniel is like me, he doesn't drink or smoke. "Oh" she says "that will suit Janet because she is very anti-alcohol because her and her mother are both Sunday school teachers, they believe alcohol is the devils butter milk and it is banned on all occasions". Just at that, Janet and Daniel walk in through the door and Marlene goes over and asked them to join them witch they did. The waiter comes over to take their order. Marlene orders garlic mushrooms for starters with salmon-en-croute for main course, James orders melon for starter with medium-to-well steak for main course. Janet orders melon for starter and smoked salmon for main course. While Daniel orders soup for starter and steak well-done.

While they wait to be served Marlene brings up the subject of religion. James wished she would talk about something else. Marlene and Daniel talk about religion as if they were two clergy preaching the gospel. Janet and James never got involved in the conversation. Marlene says to Daniel "how does your family feel about you are going out with a protestant?" Daniel says "they wouldn't know nor care. I could throw myself in front of a bus and I don't think they would notice". Marlene then says "Janet, did you tell your family yet that you are going out with a Catholic?" Janet blushes, looks down at the table and shakes her head. Her face was so red James thought she was going to break down and start crying. Neither Daniel or Marlene noticed Janet was hurting. To change the subject James says "Marlene's father is not too pleased with Marlene going out with me". Janet lifts her head, looks at James and says "how do feel about Robert not wanting you going out with Marlene?" James says "I couldn't care less about him, it's Marlene's decision and anyway that's his problem.

James was glad when the waiter arrived with the order because it changed the conversation. The waiter set the four starters on the table. Marlene, Daniel and James tuck into their starters. Janet just pushed her starter around the plate but doesn't eat any. James could see Janet was still upset so to lift her up, James thought he would tell a Brendan Grace joke. "Do you want to hear a joke Robert told me?" Everyone listened to hear what he was going to say, because they knew that Robert didn't tell jokes, and that Robert and James didn't speak very much. James continued "there was a bank robbery in Belfast. Police were looking for two men to help them with enquiries, preferably two fully qualified detectives. There's a hole on the left-hand lane of the M1 motorway, and police are looking into it". Everyone laughed, and it seemed to lift Janet. The waiter serves the main course. They tuck in and talk about the food and everything in general. James thought his meal was very nice and he was enjoying the company. They finished the main course and ordered desert. Marlene, Janet and Daniel ordered pavlova while James ordered sherry trifle. The meal was lovely, and everyone was happy with it. Daniel and James paid for the meal and they left the hotel.

They travelled over to the Ardrone Theatre and enjoyed a good show. When the show was over, James thanked Janet and Daniel for their company as they went their separate ways. On their way home Marlene says "Janet says she is madly in love with Daniel". James says "Daniel is in love with Janet too, you would know to look at them". Marlene says "I wonder how that will go down with Janet's mother Liz and her father William, with Daniel being a Catholic. Liz will kill her." As James had a great night he suddenly says "that's not our problem". James takes his left hand off the steering wheel and reaches over and catches Marline by the right hand and holds it and says "I am in love too", Marlene gives a chuckle and says "who with?" It wasn't the answer James was expecting, so he says "with myself". Marlene says "I thought so". James went quiet as he didn't know what to say. Marlene must have noticed. She says "we will listen to some music" and let go of his hand and reaches over and turns on the radio. She changed the stations until she found some music they liked. They drove to Marlene's house. Marlene wanted him to come in for a cup of tea. James refused as he was tired in which she under stood. James asked to see her again and she said yes. They arranged to meet again at the weekend as her and Janet were going back to a Belfast University tomorrow evening. As James drove down the road home he could have kicked himself for saying he was in love, as they were only going out a short space of time. But it was the truth.

On the following Friday night, James drove up to Marlene's house. He parked the car and as he got out of the car Margaret opens the door and says "come on in James". He walks up to the door and followed Margaret into the sitting room. She says "Marlene is not long home and she is not ready yet, she will be ready in a minute". James walks into the sitting room and Robert is sitting there in full RUC uniform watching television. James looks at him and the sight of that uniform turns his stomach. There was no way he could sit in the same room as an RUC man. He turns and says to Margaret "I am sorry, I will wait in the car as I want to hear something on the radio" as he walks out of the room and back to the car to wait for Marlene.

A short time later Marlene comes out of the house looking as beautiful as ever and when she gets into the car and gives James that smile his heart gives a flutter. As they drive down the road towards the town Marlene asks why he did not wait in the house. James explained that he could not sit in the same room as an RUC man, she said she under stood and that in future when he was coming to the house she would make sure that her father would take off his uniform before he arrived. James says "no you can't do that, as it is his house. The problem with the uniform is mine not his" and she agreed.   They agreed that in future that James would go into the kitchen and wait as Robert very seldom went into the kitchen.

That night they went to the cinema and enjoyed a good movie. When they came out of the cinema they went to a café and had two fish suppers. James then drove Marlene home. On the way home, James was never as happy in his life because Marlene was willing to tell her father to take of his uniform to please him. James and Marlene kept seeing each other two or three times a week and he was madly in love with her. James introduced Marlene to his mother Mary and her and Mary got on well together. As with Daniel and Janet, they were getting on well together and any one that knew them could see they were made for each other and were madly in love. Marlene and Janet were not into any sports. Daniel and James introduced them to hill climbing, table tennis and cycling and they enjoyed watching Daniel and James play football.

One July evening, James had been away on some business and had just arrived home when he got a phone call from Marlene. She seemed to be very upset. She says "you may come quick, Daniel has been arrested by the police!" James could not believe what he was hearing because Daniel never got into trouble with any one. He drove straight to Marlene's house. When James arrived, there was a police car sitting in front of the house. Daniel was sitting in the back seat. He looked terrible sitting staring straight forward. Marlene was standing outside with Margaret standing in the door way crying. Before James could speak, Marlene started "Daniel and Janet arrived here and when they arrived Janet was crying and the next thing the police arrived and wanted to speak to Daniel. Daniel went out and spoke to them. I don't know what they said. Next thing we saw was the police man putting Daniel into the back of the police car." James says "where is Janet now?" Marlene says "the police are talking to her in the upper room." They stand beside the police car talking until a police man comes out of the house and comes down to the car. James asks could he speak to Daniel. He says "no you cannot as he is under arrest". James never saw Daniel as scared looking in his life he was like a rabbit caught in a trap. A second police car arrives at the house. When the second police car arrives the first car leaves with Daniel inside.

Margaret shouts "come into the house". Marlene goes into the house followed by James. His stomach churning and his head splitting wondering what sort of a handling Daniel had got himself into. They walk into the sitting room. Robert was sitting in his chair with the telly switched off. James says hello to Robert. He looks at him and nods his head. James sits down saying nothing, knowing by the look of Robert he was as annoyed as James was about what was happening. They sit there not speaking until Margaret comes back into the room and says the police are leaving now and Marlene is with Janet. Margaret leaves the room. Robert and James don't speak a word. Margaret arrives with a tray with tea and biscuits for Robert, James and herself. James takes a cup of tea but no biscuits as he felt sick. Robert takes the tea and a biscuit and says "where are the girls?" Margaret sits down and says "the police are away and Marlene and Janet are up in the bedroom. Janet is very upset, the left side of her face is very black". Robert's hatred for Catholic's surfaces as he says "that fenian has beat her up!" Margaret tells him to be quiet. At that a horrible thought comes into James' mind "what if Daniel has hit her?" He felt like running out of the house and crying. He had known Daniel all his life and now he felt disgusted wile thinking how he could hit Janet as she loved him so much.

They sat and waited for news of what happened for a long time nobody speaking. Margaret was worried sick. Eventually Marlene entered the room. Margaret stands up and says "how's Janet?" Marlene says "she will be all right she is in my bed and she is staying here tonight. The police wanted her to go to hospital but she refused and they are sending a social worker out to see her tomorrow morning". James says "what happened to her?" Marlene says "her and her mother had a row and her mother hit her. When she realised what she had done, she phoned the police and said Daniel hit her. Margaret says "Robert, what will happen now?" Robert says "the police will put Daniel in A cell and keep him until tomorrow and charge him with assault. It will all depend on what Janet says and what Liz says". James rises from the chair and says "it's time I was going home". He says good night to Robert and Margaret. Marlene walks with him to the car. She puts her arms around him and they cuddle for a while. He then kisses her and gets into the car and leaves for home. On his way home, he breaks down and cries. When he gets home, he goes to bed and tries to sleep but can't, so he tries to pray for Daniel lying in a police cell.

Next morning, he sleeps in until half nine. He wakes up, leaps out of bed, runs to the bathroom washes, shaves and put on his clothes. He grabs some breakfast. His Mother says "what's wrong with you Jimmy? Are you not going to work today?" James says "no I am not well, my head's splitting" and he tells her about Daniel. She says you better go over and tell Daniel's Mother and Father because Daniel will need a solicitor. He says "you're right, I will go over now and tell them." He drove over to Daniel's house. As he got out of the car, Daniel's mother Molly came out of the house. James asked her was Daniel home and Molly says "Daniel never came home last night but he arrived home about half an hour ago. He washed, then spent a long time on the phone talking to that girl. Then he went out, got into the car and left". James told her what had happened she says "I knew something was wrong because I made him some breakfast and he left and never touched it". "For anyone to hit that nice girl they should get jail. I am very fond of Janet. Daniel wouldn't hit Janet because he worships her and anyway Daniel wouldn't hit a fly". James said good bye to Molly and drove home. When he arrived home his mother says "Marlene was phoning looking for you". James says "that's all right I will phone her now".

James phones Marlene. She tells him that she had spoken to Daniel and Janet and that they had told her all that had happened the night before. Janet told her mother and Father George that her and Daniel were going to get married. Liz says "you can't marry a catholic". Janet says "I love

Daniel and he's a catholic and I am going to marry him", and Liz goes into hysterics and attacks Janet with her two fists and Daniel steps in and pushes her away from Janet. Ruth reaches for the kitchen brush and starts to batter Daniel. George had to restrain her. While George was holding her, Janet and Daniel ran to the car with Liz screaming at them and as they drove of while Liz was screaming and battering the car. Daniel drove straight here and then the police arrived.

James asks "where are they now?" Marlene says "they both drove off together and never said where they were going or never said when they will be back." James said "I will call over and see Daniel later" and left it at that. Later that evening James drove over to Daniel's house to speak to Daniel. When he arrived Daniel's Mother Molly was there and invited him in. He went into the house and sat down. Mary started making tea. James asked her where Daniel was, and she says "Daniel went away this morning and came back again with Janet. I invited Janet into the house, but she refused and sat in the car. Daniel packed some clothes, put them into the car and said he was going away for a while and drove off". James told Mary all he knew as he thought she had a right to know. James thought to himself "typical Daniel spoilt rotten by his mother and thinks about nobody only himself".

James left Daniel's house and drove up to Marlene's house as he had more to do than run after Daniel. He was heading off with Marlene tomorrow morning to America for two weeks holiday. Next morning James and Marlene drive down to Shannon airport. They were to board the plane at ten am and travel to New York and get a connecting flight down to Philadelphia. When they arrive their flight is delayed. They wait around the airport for six hours before their plane takes off. When they arrive over New York, their flight is diverted to Boston due to a thunder storm. When they land in Boston it is too late for flights to Philadelphia, so the flight company puts them up for the night in a hotel. Marlene and James have a good night in a five-star hotel at the expense of the airline. Next morning a taxi picks them up at the hotel and drives them back to the airport. When they arrive back at the airport, their flight is delayed due to a wind storm in Philadelphia. James gets talking to two American marines on their way home to Philadelphia. One of the marines says to James "if I had a car I would drive down to Philly". James says "how long would it take to drive down?", the marine says "no longer than four hours". James says "I am going to hire a car and drive down". The marine says "if you are going to hire a car, we will share the expense and travel down along with you". James hires a big Jeep for a week. James, Marlene and the two marines set of for Philadelphia with James driving. The marines introduce themselves as Vincent and Shaun. Marlene says "Shaun and Vincent are very Irish names". Shaun says "my father is from Monaghan and my mother is from Donegal". Vincent says "my father is from county Kerry". As they reached the outskirts of Philly, James says "we would need to look for a hotel". Shaun says "there's a very good hotel very near where I live. You could book in there and we will walk you home". As they were talking Vincent says "my girlfriend is from Strabane county Tyrone, her name is Sara".

When they arrived at the hotel, the two Marines offered James money but James refused. The marines said they would make it up to them. The marines went on their way, and James and Marlene booked into the hotel. As they were very tired from traveling, they went to bed as soon as they booked in. Next morning they were up early to have their breakfast. When they finish their breakfast, Marlene goes back up to her room to get her coat to go out, as James waits in the foyer. While James is waiting, Vincent arrives in with his girlfriend. He introduces her to James as Sara and says "we are here to take you out and show you Philly". Marlene arrives and is introduced to Sara. Vincent leads the way as they leave the hotel. Vincent says, we will take the train into the city centre. Sara says "Shaun and Vincent are going to give you the holiday of your life". Marlene and Sara get on so well together you would think they knew each other all their life. James thought "that's my Marlene, she could get on well with any one".

They the train into the city centre. They leave the train station and walk to the liberty bell. They visit the liberty bell with its crack, visit the seat of the first American government, and do a guided tour of the building and hear about how the government and the courts worked and why the government moved from Philadelphia to Washington. They visit the ship that carried home the unknown soldier from France. They go down into a second world war submarine, they visit the F. B. I. headquarters. They decided they would look for something to eat, Vincent says "we will go down China town and we will get something to eat there". James was in two minds as he didn't like Chinese food. They walk into a small restaurant and take their seats. There were no other customers in the restaurant. A middle-aged coloured lady comes over to them with the menu. She hands a menu to James, he takes the menu and says to the lady "if your husband was out working all day and had nothing to eat, what would you give him when he arrived home? Well that's what I want now". The woman laughs and says "that's fine" and takes back the menu. The others order a meal while the waiter talks to James about Ireland. She said she learned a lot about Ireland. The only thing she could not understand was what turf was. James explains what turf is and the waitress leaves with their order. The waitress arrives back with their order and sets it on the table. They enjoy their meal and James thinks it was the nicest meal he ever had. James and Vincent pay for the meal. They each give the waitress twenty dollars to show their appreciation.

They take the train back to their hotel. When they arrive back at the hotel, Vincent says "be up early in the morning because we have a lot to see". Sara asks "when are you going home?" James says "we are flying out on Sunday". Sara says "that gives us plenty of time". Sara says "the Philadelphia GAA are holding a Tyrone banquet on Wednesday night in the Irish centre, would you like to go?" James says "we would love to go". Next morning Vincent and Sara are waiting for them with a car. When they are ready, Vincent drives them out of town. He drives them down as far as Gettysburg to see the battlefield. James and Marlene couldn't believe how big the battlefield was. They spend the day in Gettysburg. Next morning Vincent drives them out to see the Amish country and the corn fields. Next day they all meet up and spend the day relaxing and playing golf. Marlene nor James were very good at golf but that didn't matter they enjoyed the day.

It was time to go back to the hotel and get ready for the banquet. Marlene and James dressed up for the banquet. They meet up with Vincent, Sara, Shaun, and Shaun's girlfriend Una. They walk into the Irish centre. James with Marlene linked on his arm, as if they were King and Queen. That's how proud they felt. As they were seated at the table, James was seated with Marlene on his right side and with Una on his left side. Una asks James what they were doing tomorrow. James says "we're flying out home from New York on Sunday morning. We are going down to Washington tomorrow and on Friday we are going to New York as we want to see New York before we go home". Una says "I am from Manhattan and I am going home on Friday morning for a week's holiday. I will travel up to New York with you and show you the sights". The banquet was fantastic. James and Marlene met and talked to so many people they had known from home they wished the banquet could last for ever. Next morning, they meet up with Vincent and Sara and travel down to Washington D.C. They See the Whitehouse and walk around the city, and find it is not very impressive. They decided to travel back to Philly, as Marlene wanted to do some shopping. Vincent drove them to a shopping mall. Marlene never saw shops anything like these shops in her life.

Early next morning, Shaun and Una pick up James and Marlene and they drive up to New York. On the way up to New York, Una says "the city will be very busy today so I rang my mother and she says we are to call round as she will have some sandwiches for us". When they arrived at Una's house Una's mother Josie had a big breakfast ready for them. They eat the breakfast, thanked Josie and drove into town. They visited the Empire State Building and climbed to the top. They hire a boat and sail down the Hudson around the Statue of Liberty under Manhattan Bridge and Brooklyn bridge. James thought it was amazing to drive over and sail under the bridges on the same day. They visit Central Park and anywhere worth seeing in New York, they saw it. They walked for miles in and out of shops. That evening when they got back to Una's house, they could not believe Josie had a three course dinner ready for them. They eat the dinner and talked a long time to Josie and her husband Patrick. When they left the house it was dark. Una stayed at home as Shaun drove them back to Philly.

Next day Vincent and Shaun drove them over to Virginia and visited Arlington military cemetery. They saw Present Kennedy's grave with the everlasting flame. They also saw the changing of the guard, and the unknown soldier's grave. They saw graves from the civil war, Korean war, Vietnam war, and the First and Second World Wars. The entire holiday was fantastic. Next morning Vincent drove them up to New York airport. Their holiday was over. Marlene and James had really enjoyed their holiday. Marlene said she never thought she would ever see America that her father and mother were never out of Northern Ireland in their entire lives.

On their way home at the airport, James got talking to a customs officer and he asked how their holiday was. James told him all the places they had seen, and he says "you have never been to America until you cross the Mississippi". James says "how far is it to the Mississippi?" The officer laughs and says "it's only three thousand miles to the Mississippi". James laughs and says "its only three thousand miles to Shannon Airport and it takes the plane nearly nine hours". It was then that James had decided when the time was right he would ask Marline to marry him and they would go back to America for their honeymoon, hire a car and spend six months traveling from New York to California. He loved Marlene so much he would have done anything for her.

James mulled over this great idea for a long time. One nice Sunday evening, after he came home from a football match his team had won, he drove up to Marlene's house as arranged. Margaret had made a nice tea ready for him. He had the tea and asked Marlene would she like to go for a walk. Marline said yes she would go for a walk. They drive up to Fermanagh Park in the car and walked up Cairn rock. It was beautiful. It is said that you can see twenty-two counties of Ireland from Cairn rock At the top of Cairn rock, they could see for miles in every direction. James dropped on one knee and asked Marlene to marry him. He never saw Marlene so excited when she said yes, they cuddled for a while and Marlene wanted to go home and tell her mother.

They drove back to Marlene's house and Marlene tells her father and mother. Margaret congratulated them, Robert congratulated Marlene, but he never acknowledged James. They then drove down to tell James' mother. On the way down, James was annoyed with Robert. Marlene said not to worry, as he would come around when he got used to the idea. When they told James mother, she was over the moon and gave Marlene a big hug and then gave James a hug. James was never as happy in his entire life. Mary says "I was waiting for this day, now," she says "I can retire and I will get a little house in the town. You can have this house and farm". Two days later, tragedy struck, when James was on his way home from work he was travelling at about fifty miles an hour along the Drumquin to Omagh road. Out of the ditch jumped a big stag. He hit the stag with his car and lost control of the car. The car rolled over the ditch and hit a big ash tree. James was badly hurt. He woke up six days later in a Belfast hospital with a broken leg and several other injuries.

When he woke up, Mary was sitting beside his bed holding his hand. He did not speak. His mother told him to go back to sleep as he was very ill. When he woke up again his mother was still there, and she told him that Marlene was in to see him several times. He was in a daze and didn't know what was happening. He kept wakening and sleeping for a couple of days. After a period, he woke up with his head clear. Marlene was sitting beside the bed and she looked as if she hadn't slept for a month. She asks James how he was. James said he was very sore but he was all right. James ask her how she was. Marlene says she was very tired and that she hadn't left the hospital for over a week. James says "you can go home now and have a good rest". She never answered. Just at that Mary arrived back into the ward. Miranda gave James a kiss and left the ward. Mary says "poor Marlene, she is worn out". James says "she will be all right, she is going home now for a rest". Mary says "she is away down to see her father first". James says "what's wrong with Robert?" Mary says "Oh, I have put my foot in it, I was not supposed to tell you. I may tell you now, Robert was on duty the night after your accident and Marlene was up sitting with you. There was a gun battle and Robert was shot in the thigh and he is in the ward down the corridor". James says "how is he?" Mary says "he had to have major surgery". She says "I went down to see him after he came out of surgery. I met Margaret, she is a lovely woman". At this stage James' mind was in turmoil. He asks his mother to leave him as he wanted to go to sleep. Mary gave him a kiss on the cheek and left. That whole night his mind was in turmoil. He could not sleep, thinking of Marlene and what she had been through and him not being there to support her. Next morning he asked the nurse could he go down to see Robert, she says "you have to ask the doctor when he comes in. If he says it's all right I will take you down".

The doctor comes in and examines James. He asks him could he go down to the other ward to see Robert. The doctor says "you are still very ill, and you are not allowed out of bed". After the doctor leaves the ward the nurse comes in and says "I will see if Robert can come to see you". About fifteen minutes later the nurse comes in wheeling Robert in a wheelchair. She leaves Robert bedside James' bed and says "I will be back in ten minutes and take you back to your ward". James did not know what to say to Robert. As he approached the bed, he reaches out his hand. Robert takes his hand and he says "how are you James". James replies "I am well, how are you?" Robert says "I will live another while". James asks "what happened to you?" Robert starts to tell him every little detail of what happened. James is happy to let Robert do all the talking. Marlene arrives into the ward and is over the moon to see James and Robert talking.

Robert feels very tired so Marlene wheels him back to the ward and helps him into bed. As soon as Robert leaves, James falls asleep. Next morning, Marlene comes in to see James. James asks her to take him down to see Robert. Marlene gets a wheelchair and helps James out of bed and into the wheelchair. She wheels James to the other ward to see Robert. James sits beside Robert's bed and falls asleep while Robert tells him the nitty gritty details of his shooting. Marlene wheels him back to the ward. It took Marlene and two nurses to put James back into bed. A nurse says "He is not sleeping, he is unconscious". The nurse sounds the alarm and calls for the doctor. The doctor   examines James and gives him an injection. James regains consciousness again and the doctor tells James not get out of bed again. His trip down to the other ward took too much out of him and had set him back. James says "I only went down to see my future father in law". The Doctor says "James, you need to realise that you are very ill. You have multiple fractures. The less movement you make the better. Don't get out of that bed for the next four days and then I will review you again. But as he is your father in law I will arrange for you to see him more often". The Doctor continued his rounds.

About one hour later James fell asleep he slept for about three hours. When he woke up Robert was sitting beside his bed. He says, "if you are going to marry my daughter you cannot lay in bed all day sleeping!" James was in agony. Robert says "the Doctor sent me up to look after you". James didn't speak because he was very sick and did not want to see Robert or anyone else, he just wanted to be left alone. Robert picked up that he wasn't well and said nothing more. James went to sleep again when he woke up it was the next day and he felt a lot better. It was only then that he learnt that the Doctor had Robert moved to the bed beside James. Robert was allowed out of bed and James wasn't. Robert talked a lot about farming, as he had been reared on a farm. He knew that as well as James' engineering job he worked on his mother's farm. Robert did everything for James from reading the newspaper to him every morning to getting him drinks or anything else he needed. Any one who came into see James, Robert would say to them that he had to look after James because James was going to make Marlene a farmer. Then he would laugh. Robert did everything he could to help every patient in the ward. The nurses loved him because he would sit, and spoon feed a patient who couldn't feed himself and any other thing he could do for the nurses. James and Robert discovered that they had a lot in common. They both enjoyed talking about farming, football, and history, among other things.

Time passed, and Robert went home. James had to stay for longer. Marlene would call to see him and as they would talk about getting married James loved to see her. After a period, James was sent home and improved slowly. Instead of James going to see Marlene, she would come to see James. Sometimes Robert and Margaret would call to see James. Mary, Marlene, Margaret, Robert and James became friends. Robert left the RUC and got his pension. He would say when James was fit he would take him and teach him how to shoot, and they could go out game shooting, which James looked forward to. By this time Marlene had qualified and got herself a job teaching in Coleraine.

After about one year, James had recovered enough to go back to work as an engineer with road services. In all this time nobody had heard from Daniel or Janet and nobody seemed to know where they were. Daniel's mother phoned James on several occasions and asked him did he know where Daniel was, but he have anything to tell her. Marlene and James set a date for their wedding. Both families were over-joyed to hear they were going to get married. James told Marlene he wanted to get married in the Catholic Church, but if she didn't, he would accept it and they would get married somewhere else. Marlene said she was happy to get married in the Catholic Church, but she was not going to change her religion. James was happy with that, because he loved her he said he didn't care what religion she was. Marlene was happy with that. James went to bed thinking about Marlene and he woke up in the morning thinking Marlene   .

James' uncle Charlie, Mary's brother, died suddenly over in Manchester. Mary asked James to go over to Manchester as she was unable to travel. This meant James leaving Marlene to arrange the wedding. He took the bus to Belfast and caught the overnight sailing on the Princess Margaret from Belfast to Liverpool. As it was a very stormy night, James got no sleep. On arriving in Liverpool at 8am, he caught the bus for Manchester. James arrived in Manchester and his cousin Edward met him at the bus station. He stayed at Edward's house and he phoned Marlene every night. After Charlie's funeral, Edward and his friends went to a pub for the funeral meal. After the meal, they all started drinking. As James didn't drink, he just moved about talking to people. He met a man named Brian from Coleraine who was over in Manchester on a course. As they got talking, James told him told him he knew a girl who was a teacher in a school in Coleraine. The man says that he knew her, she teaches in the school his children go to, and his oldest girl was in her class. Brian told James that Marlene was going out with a colleague. James was rocked to the ground when he was told that Marline was going out with someone else, as they had set the date for their wedding.

James thought to himself "no way, not my Marlene, she loves me!" For the next three days and nights, his mind was in turmoil. He can't wait to get home. He doesn't phone Marlene because he did not know what to say to her. James catches the bus and travels up to Liverpool on Saturday afternoon. He catches the overnight sailing from Liverpool to Belfast. He travels second class on the Princess Margaret. It was a calm night and the sailing was very smooth. James spent most of the night standing out on deck looking into the water. He arrives in Belfast at 8am and waited for the eleven o' clock bus to Omagh. James arrives in Omagh abought one in the afternoon. There was no bus to Fintona on a Sunday, and there was only one taxi in the town. The taxi owner and his wife ran the taxi from a confectionary shop in Bridge Street. James walked to the shop and asked for the taxi. The shop keeper says to James "the taxi is out collecting a fare He will be dropping them off in front of the hotel in Main Street in ten minutes if you want to go over to the front of the hotel and wait there". James buys a bar of chocolate and walks over to main street, he stands in the door way of the drapery shop next to the hotel. He opens the chocolate and starts to eat it, as he stood there in in the shop doorway, waiting and eating his chocolate. A man comes out of the hotel stands in the doorway after a few seconds Marline comes out of the hotel takes the man by the hand, James can't believe what he was seeing, he takes a step back so that Marline won't see him. The man and Marline walk down the street holding hands for about thirty yards to a parked car Marline gets into the front passenger seat of the car and the man gets into the driver's seat and they drive up the street past where James is standing. James stands there in shock until the taxi arrives James gets into the taxy hart broken, he tells the taxi driver to take him home. The taxi driver says to him are you all right you're like a man that should be going to Hospital not home. James said I am all right I came over on the boat from Liverpool last night and I got no sleep.

When James arrived home, Mary says Marlene was phoning looking for you and she said she would phone you later. James said if she phones again tell her I do not want to speak to her I am going up to bed for a rest. As James went out of the living room door the phone rang guessed it was Marlene, he stood outside the door listened to his mother on the phone, he could hear her say he's away up to bed and I don't know what's wrong with him, you couldn't speak to him because he's like a bear with a sore head. He left at that and walked up the stairs and lay down on top of the bed clothes and cried, as he lay on top of the bed crying the phone rang again, and he heard his mother answer it. Next Mary hung up the phone opened the living room door and shouted Jimmy Marlines coming down to see you. James just lay there closed his eyes with the world going around in his head. he fell asleep. Next thing he heard his mother shouting Jimmy Marline here. James gets up from the bed goes down stairs to the living room. Mary says Marline is waiting in the car she wouldn't come in.

James goes out opens the passenger door of the car gets into the car and closes the door and says drive away from here Marline says what's wrong. James say's as she drives off there's far too much wrong.

She drives to the car park at the local football club and parks there. Marline says what's wrong James says you tell me what's wrong who the man was you were sitting in the car with in Omagh today She says who told you that he says i saw you myself. Marline says that wasn't me. James says I saw you myself James thought she couldn't figure out how he saw her, so she denied up and down that she was ever in Omagh today. James couldn't understand why she was denying it so much. James then says what about this fellow John you are going out with in Coleraine. Marline says john is a colleague and from the first day I started in the school he took a fancy to me but I am not interested in him and never went out with him ever.   , he ask me out on several occasions and I refused because I was engaged to you

                                                                While you were in Manchester my car broke down and was in the garage When I got a message that daddy had taken a heart attack and was in hospital. I had no way of getting home so John volunteered to drive me home which I accepted. When he drove me up he decided he would stay overnight. I went to see daddy and when I came home from Hospital he phoned and said he was staying in the hotel in Enniskillen and ask me to join him for a meal and I said yes and he drove out to the house and picked me up and I joined him for a meal which I saw no harm in I suppose he was a shoulder to cry on. James sat there and listened to Marline crying and apologise he listened for a long time to her crying and asking him to forgive her James says I am sorry Marline I can't trust you and opened the car door and got out and walked up the car park walked home and left Marline sitting there in the carpark crying.

Next evening Monday Marline phoned James and said I went today and says to Brian where did you get the idea that I was going out with John Brian says he saw John at a parents teacher meeting and he told him that he was going out with me and when I tackled John it seems that Brian wasn't the only one he told that he was going out with me James says Marline what about the man in Omagh Marline says there was no man In Omagh because I was never in Omagh that day James says it's too late Marline it's all over and hung up the phone.

That night James didn't sleep thinking about Marline, the man in Omagh kept going over and over in his mind all night, Next day James expected Marline to phone he thought to himself when she phones I will forgive her because he missed her but Marline didn't phone. James was feeling so bad he didn't go to work for two weeks waiting for Marline to phone him he still loved her he had got it into his head that she was in the wrong and she should come back to him and apologise. he was so stubborn he wouldn't call her. If she had called the next day or the days after he would have said forget about it I am sorry but she never called. Three month later he heard that Robert had died, he sent Margaret a sympathy card.

Almost two years passed, and never heard from Marlene and thought he had got over her and was working on the road in Omagh. The work men were using stop and signs and James was measuring some work when a wedding party drove past. The bride waved at him and he could have sworn it was Marline. he felt sick and had to go home. For two weeks he could not get Marline out of his mind he decided it was time for him to call Marline as she wasn't going to call him. He phoned the house Margaret answered he did not say who he was and ask to speak to Marline Margaret says Marline not here she will not be back for two weeks as she got married and is away on honey moon. James cried and cursed himself as it was all his own fault he still loved Marline and now it was too late he had driven her into the arms of someone else.

Time passed Mary died nobody ever heard from Danial Janet nor Marline and James never felt as lonely in his life with a good job a good car and plenty of money in the bank and now I am living was on his own. James had a nervous brake down and was in and out of hospital and seeing councillors for years he read in the paper that Marlines mother had died he would have loved to go and comfort Marline, but he couldn't go. Danial's mother and father both died. And never found out where Danial was. Every time James met Moly the first words she would say to him was did you ever hear from Danial and he would have to say no and the whole conversation would be about Danial. James went to their wakes and funerals Danial never turned up and no one had heard from him or knew where he was.

Thirty years passed James lived on his own and never looked at another girl since himself and Marline parted company. he still loved Marline and thought about her every day, but he never heard anything from her or where she was. he never heard from Danial or Janet. For all knew they could all be dead. He buried himself in his engineering job and did some charity work. and some farming. Things were changing very fast in Northern with infer structure changing North and South. James had to travel up to Dublin for an engineering conference. he was now into his fifties and thinking of taking early retirement.   James arrived in Dublin at about nine a.m. took the Louis to the hotel where the conference was taking place, booked in for the three nights of the conversance which wasn't due to start until Eleven a.m. he met up with some people he had met before and they went to gather and had some breakfast.

When they arrived in the conference hall the conference was about to start. They took their seats immediately. As soon as they sat down the first speaker started to speak James wasn't very much interested in what he was saying as he had heard it all before. He felt like shouting up to him to tell us something we didn't now. This was another conference to justify men in government departments big salaries. He was sitting their bored to death. The conference broke for lunch when the first speaker finished.

He had lunch and came back into the hall when the second speaker took the podium it was nearly two o clock he took his seat as the second speaker was starting to speak. James wasn't paying much attention as he was reading some literature. When he looked up he could not believe what my eyes was seeing. There standing at the podium talking was Danial.   His mind went straight back over thirty years. All the good times we had all those years ago from the day we started primary school in 1953 until the day we met Janet and Marline. James waited the rest of that evening to get a chance to speak to Danial wondering where he was all these years and what he had been doing and where was Janet and what had happened to her.

That evening when the conference finished James went up and approached Danial when Danial saw James he put his arms around him and they gave each other a big hug. They didn't get much time to talk as Danial had a busy schedule. Danial ask James to meet him later when the conference finished for the day. and stay at his house overnight, James refused refused as he had arranged to meet some people in the hotel for dinner. They arranged to meet up the next day at lunch break to catch up on the past.

Next day at lunch break they met up and went for lunch to gather

Danial talked ninety to the dozen James could not get in a word in edgeways. After a while Danial settled down when he got over the excitement of meeting James again. Danial told James he and Janet were madly in love and that too many people were interfering and the incident with Janet's mother was the last straw and they ran away. He says Liz told the police enough Lies to hang me and the police believed her because I was a catholic and George and Liz were staunch loyalists. James asked about Janet and what happened to her. Danial says we got married and lived happily ever after. They now had three growing up sons two which were doctors and one was a solicitor and one daughter who was a schoolteacher, and Danial was a professor in trinity college' Janet had retired from teaching He told James that the day that they left Tyrone was the best of his life as he and Janet were both Millionaires. When they got married they bought a small house with fifteen acres of land on the out skirts or the city. Five years ago, it was designated development land. and they had just sold it for fifteen million Punts and bought a new house. Danial wanted James to stay for a few days. As James had the farm to look after he could not stay. James told Danial all about Marline. James promised Danial he would come up whenever he retired for a week.

James told Danial that his mother and Father had died, and it he seemed he couldn't care less. James came home every now and again he phoned Danial they would talk for ages. Danial never phoned James, so James stopped phoning Danial. Contact between them stopped once more.

Years passed, and he never heard from Danial for over ten years, when out of the blue James got a card from Janet inviting him to a seventy's surprise birthday party in a Dublin hotel for Danial. James phoned the hotel immediately and booked a room to stay for three nights.   When the date arrived, James drove up to Dublin and arrived early booked into the hotel. There was a sit-down meal set for six thirty p.m. James went up to his room lay on the bed and watched television until it was time to get ready.

James took a shower shaved and dressed up in his best suit with white shirt and his red and black tie. he went down to the foyer and was ushered into a room where there were a table set for about ten people. There was already a man and woman sitting at the table. All places at the table were named James looked at the labels found his seat and sat down. His seat was the seat beside Danial. James introduced himself to the man and women at the table. Then two more men arrived with two woman and took their seats. Everyone seemed to know each other except for James. he Sat there and listened to them. Then a woman walked through the door he couldn't believe it was no other than Marline she took her seat beside James as his heart started to flutter. He said hello to Marline she turned her head round and said hello she hadn't noticed it was James she was as surprised as James was and didn't know what to say.

Next Janet and Danial entered the room, and everyone started to sing happy birthday Danial. The meal was very nice. Thank god that Janet and Marline talked a lot during the meal. Because James didn't know what to say. Everyone at the table seemed to be strangers to James he only knew Danial Janet and Marline, it was over forty years since he had a serious conversation with any of them. He was starting to regret coming.

The arrangements were that the party would go to the theatre after the meal. James made the excuse that he was very tired and that he would fall asleep in the theatre and anyway he didn't like the theatre Marline made her excuses that she was tired and didn't want to go to the theatre either.

James went up to his bedroom wishing he could be alone with Marline. He didn't know what Marline was thinking but Janet was thinking which was far from my thinking. When they all left for the theatre James went out bought himself the daily newspaper and took up a seat in the hotel foyer and started to read his paper after about half an hour as he was sitting reading his paper when he looked up and there was Marline standing beside him. Marline says it's a long evening with nothing to do only watch television James says yes, it is , Marline says I was just going to order a cup o tea will you join me James says I will. James stands up and Marline says sit where you are and I will order it. Marline went into the bar and ordered two teas and toast with butter and marmalade jam. And ask the barman to bring the tea out to the foyer Marline paid the barman went back to James and sat down facing James. James looked at Marline she looked as nice as the first time he had saw her. Marline says what did you think of the party, James the meal was very nice, but I felt very uncomfortable everyone there were strangers to me. Marline Janet set this up to get you and me to gather, how did she know about us/ Janet contacted me on face book about five years ago and we have been in contact ever since and I told her all about what happened between us, so she set us up tonight, you and I not going to the theatre and meeting here is just pure accidental. Believe me I had nothing to do with it, I didn't know you were coming I was looking forward to Janet and myself getting together and her and me could catch up on old times. Marline says what have you been up to all these years James says, not very much Just working and sleeping, at that the waiter came with the tea and toast. Marline gives that lovely smile and looks at the tea and says how lovely I am just choking for a nice cup of tea. James O you haven't forgot I love marmalade.

Well Marline what have you been up to since the last time I saw you, where do you want me to start James was starting to enjoy this and said cheekily you may start at the beginning. She started well you know I never got married to after you left I don't know what to do I still loved you. I thought had got over you until daddy died I thought you would have came up. Why am I telling you all this it's all behind me now, go on Marline I want to know because I still love you Marline gives a smile and continues, When you didn't call I gave up, i knew my marring you was over I still loved you and always will I buried myself in my work, and kept thinking of you. I never looked at another fella again. James listens and says sorry marline. Why did you go out with john in the first place? I was getting married and John fancied me bigtime I decided I would go out with him just to satisfy myself that I was doing the right thing getting married. The last fling if you know what I mean. I was only when I was out with John that I knew how much I loved you.   Nobody will know how much I loved you. I was prepared to tell you all about John when the time was right somebody told you first and when you brought it up I didn't know what to say because I was so surprised that you knew, people should keep their big mouths shut.

Why did you not phone me after that night we parted Marline when you stepped out of the car and walked away it seemed to me so final, I sit there in the car and cried for an hour hopping you would come back, and you never came. Believe me I wanted to call you, I didn't go to work for three days. Marline anyway, why didn't you phone. I did phone, but it was too late you were married, Marline mammy was right she said some one phoned and she thought it was you, but you hung up before she could ask who it was. IF I had been sure that it was you who phoned I would have phoned you back. That evening when mammy told me that you phoned It would have taking very little for me to come running to you. James is sitting there thinking how foolish he had been and messed everything up.

Marline says what do you mean me being married James when I saw your wedding party go through Omagh I was hart broken and phoned your mother and she said you were away on two weeks holiday I thought you were away on honey moon. Marline laughs and says honey moon I would need to get married first. James you say you never married what happened Marline you left me. James I saw you dressed as the bride in Omagh Marline here we go again me being I in Omagh again when I was never in Omagh .James sat there not knowing what to say, stands up and says its bed time Marline says sit down James sits down, Marline says you must be the best man in the world for jumping to conclusions, James sits there quiet as Marline carries on I was never in Omagh that day and I was never in a wedding dress, James I don't understand. Marline I do understand She informs James that Before Robert died he told her he had an affair with a police college in Omagh and that she got pregnant and had a baby girl. Marline i had a half-sister living with her mother in Omagh I looked her up and we met. When we met I couldn't believe it I and my half-sister Miranda were nearly the same age and were like twins. It had to be her that you saw Marline I never forgave Robert because he got that wo0man pregnant when mammy was pregnant with me.

James again stands up and says its time for bed as I have so much to take in, Marline stands up as James walks around the coffee table she reaches her arms out and automatedly James puts his arms around her and give her a cuddle as he hold her tight as tears comes to his eyes, he don't want to let her go as he feels like crying. He holds her a long time, he lets her go and says I will see you in the morning and leave s to go up to his room James gets into bed and lies half the night thinking about the life he had missed with Marline and by now should have been living with Marline and a growing up family.   Next morning, James gets up early gets ready and goes down to the dining room for breakfast. When he finishes Breakfast James goes outside for a good walk he, bought the morning paper, went back to the hotel, sat down in the foyer and started to read his paper with the corner of his eye he saw Marline come out of the dining room after having her breakfast I he waved to her and she came straight over gave me that smile bent down and gave him a kiss on the lips it was almost fifty years since the last time she had kissed him. James smiles and says that was nice and says you were the last person to kiss me nearly fifty years ago Marline says nothing sits down beside James takes his hand in her two hands and starts to massage his hand. They both sit there for along time saying nothing. James never felt so much in love in his entire life and knew Marline felt the same.   James was the first to speak Marline I enjoyed your company last night and I am so happy to meet up with you again this morning. Marline says I enjoyed your company and I still love you as much as ever. James smiled and held her hand tight and felt sixteen again. The manager of the hotel seen them or someone told him. Because a waiter came over and set tea and toast on the table in front of Marline and James and says compliments of the hotel.

They drank the tea and eat the toast Marline says I am so happy James says get your coat and we will go for a walk as I think everyone is looking at us Marline stands up and says I don't care about them and goes to her room to get her coat, she came back wearing her coat James thought she was looking as lovely as she was the first time he saw her. James lifts his coat from the back of the chair went to put it on Marline takes his coat holds it for him he slips hiss arms into the sleeves straighten it Butten's it Marline hooks her arm into James arm as they walk out the door as proud as a peacocks.

They walk up the street visit the G.P. O. take a sight seeing trip of the city as far out as Glasnevin Cemetery and the Botanic gardens they sit in the café in the Botanic gardens with a cup of tea when marline reached across the small table takes James by the hand and says Jimmy I know I am no spring chicken, but I love you so much and time is short will you marry me. James looked at her across the table into those lovely green eyes and thought for a long time and didn't know what to say and thought of all the times he had thought of marrying Marline. James says Marline I love you so must do you realise I am over Seventy years of age now' Marline says It doesn't matter what age you are I still want to marry you. At that James felt like crying. James rises from the table walks out the door up the garden followed by Marline he stops in front of the rose bushes and weights for Marline to catch up Marline says I am sorry

James put his arm around her waist and pulls her close to him and says with a heavy heart no Marline I am sorry it is too late and she agrees. He held her tight for a while then they walk down to the bus no words spoken until they get on the bus to go back to their hotel. It Was late when they arrived back to the hotel when they arrived back we had a nice dinner and retired for the night. James lay in bed that night and couldn't sleep at the thought of not seeing Marline again he thought he would go insane.

He was up early next morning because had planned to go to Tipperary to stay with some friends for a few days James had planned to catch the nine o'clock express train from Dublin to Cork. James sat in the dinning room of the hotel with his breakfast sitting in front of him he was not fit to eat it as he couldn't get Marline out of his mind and wondering if he would ever see her again. Marline had planned to go home that morning.

Just when James was about to leave the table Marline comes in through the door he watches her until she gets her breakfast and sits down at a table he couldn't stand watching her any longer he rises from his table and walks over to Marlines table take her by the hand drops down on one knee and says Marline will you marry me Marline puts her arms around his shoulders and gives him a kiss and says yes and every one in the dining room start to clap.

James goes over to his table lifts his breakfast carries it over to Marlines table sets it down and sits down opposite Marline to eat his breakfast. As they eat their breakfast James looked at Marline and says this is the best I have made. Marline says yes, I am so happy I could cry. James says don't cry because you look so beautiful Marline laughs. As the other guests finished their breakfast and were leaving the dining room the all congratulated James and marline. One woman around Marlines age said to Marline you are so lucky I wish my man would ask me to marry him.

When James and Marline were finishing their breakfast, the hotel Manager approached them and presented marline with a voucher for a dinner bed and breakfast for tonight. When they left the dining room, James says I would need to go up to my room and pack to go to Tipperary, Marline will you come to Tipperary with me Marline nods her head and says I will Meet you down here in half an hour. I want to phone Janet and tell her my good news James smiles gives her a kiss on the cheek and leaves to go to his room.

James packs takes his suit case goes down to the foyer to check out when he went to check out he changed his mind and decided he would wait until Marline was checking out and pay for the two of them. He takes a seat in the lobby to wait for Marline. As he's waiting in through the door comes Janet and Danial they stand and look around James stands up as he stands up Janet runs over and throws her arms around him and congratulates him. Danial shakes James hand and gives him a hug, Janet says where's Marline/James Marline up in her room packing we are going to Tipperary she will be down in a minute. Danial there will be no Tipperary this week as you are our guests.

Just at that Marline enters the lobby Janet runs over and nearly lifts her of her feet. The two men just there as Marline drops her suit case and puts her arms around Janet, the women hold each other tight no words spoken they both cry. James is so happy he walks out side to keep from crying Danial follows him out are you all right says Danial James it's just that I am so proud of Marline. Danial puts a reassuring arm around James as they go back into the hotel to join the woman. Danial gives Marline a cuddle and congratulates her. Marline says we would soon need to go if we are going to Tipperary to day Danial says no you are not going to Tipperary to day you are staying with us and that's that. Danial goes over to the receptionist talks to her the receptionist speaks on the phone and then talks to Danial again the hotel manager for a long time. He then comes back to James and marline and says that's it leave your bags back to your rooms you are staying another two nights with us. Danial had booked them into the hotel for another two nights. James and Marline leave their bags back up to the same rooms and come down to join Danial and Janet,

When they arrive back to the hotel lobby Danial has a small lunch ordered for them in the dining room, the four of them enjoy the lunch and cant stop talking They leave the hotel Janet and David show them around Dublin city they walk around the city for a couple of hours arrive back to the hotel about four P.M. Order tea and sit in the hotel foyer drinking tea and talking until dinner time. They go into the dining room have their dinner and talk for a long time Danial and James couldn't believe how much they had to catch up on. They agreed to meet up again next morning and parted company for the night When Janet and Danial left for home James says that's good I never hardly got talking to you today Marline says I enjoyed catching up with Janet and I am looking forward to meeting her tomorrow again. James and marline gave each other a kiss and a cuddle and parted for the night.

Next morning Marline joined James for breakfast when they finished breakfast and came out of the dinning room Danial was sitting in the lobby of the hotel waiting for them. They join Danial and leave the hotel go with Danial to Danial's house where Janet is waiting Danial says that he would show them all round Co. Meath today, Janet says she can't go out as she has a very sore foot she will stay at home Marline says to James you and Danial go and I will stay with Janet. They agreed that Danial and James would go for a game of golf. James and Danial left for the golf club Marline says let me see that foot Janet says there's very little wrong with my foot, I only wanted the men away out of the road so that I could get talking to you without them interrupting. Marline laughs and says Janet you will never change. Janet says Marline we are going to have a great day because I haven't had a good laugh since we were together in Tyrone .

Marline says Janet when you left and James left and daddy died I wished I were dead Janet put her arms around her and they cried Marline told Janet all about James seeing her half-sister Ruby in Omagh and thinking it was her. Janet, I didn't know you had a sister Marline I didn't either until I told daddy about James saying he saw me in Omagh with another man and breaking of our engagement just before daddy died it was then that he said he had an affair with a college. Marline told Janet everything about James and her whole life Janet told Marline How tough it was when her and Danial ran away, and she would do it all over again because her and Danial were so much in love and were so happy. Janet told Marline stories about her mother Liz the way she used to beat her for nothing and that she treated her father badly and she didn't care about her father because he ran about being a big Orange man with his hard hat and sash and never stood up and defended her once it was her brother who told them that she was going out with a catholic and that her brother William was worse than her mother and father together. She said that night she left they beat her so badly before Danial arrived and only Danial came when he came they might have killed me. Danial had to hit

William as hard as he could to get me out of the house and away from them. Janet told Marline that when her and Danial got to Dublin she thought she was going to die and that Danial took her to hospital and that she had a damaged spleen and spent the week in hospital. The hospital reported it to the Garda and that two garda inter viewed her. the guards said would put out a warrant for Williams arrest. When the Garda contacted the R.U.C. the R.U.C. told them that it was Danial who beat me. Janet where is William now Marline I don't know when your Mother and father died he sold the farm and went away to Belfast. I heard that he got involved with the U.V.F. he served a time in prison and when he got out of prison he went to Scotland and nobody seems to know where he is. Marline asks Janet to be her brides maid Janet agrees and says to marline it I can't believe I am going to be a brides maid I am seventy years of age and I was never at a wedding in my life other than my own. Janet puts her arms around Marlines shoulders and says Marline you always made me so happy and I missed you so much all these years.

James and Danial walked around the golf course all day and talked about everything Danial told James all about him Janet and Janet's family and that he left home and never made contact since he left because he was afraid of the police He told James about hitting William and that William and liz were one in the same very wicket people James asked Danial to be best man and Danial said he would be honoured to be best man for him and Marline James says you must admit we led interesting lives

When James and Danial arrive back at the house Janet had booked four dinners in the hotel for them They agreed to meet one hour from now in the foyer of the hotel for Dinner James and Marline walked back to the hotel to get ready for dinner. On their way back to the hotel the conversation was all ab out Janet and William Marline said she knew William all her life and that she never liked him and that she now knew why Janet spent so much time at her house if Margaret and Robert had known that liz were beating her they would have taken her in and looked after her. When they arrived back at the hotel Marline and James went to their rooms to get ready for dinner.   When they were ready they came back down to the lobby to wait for Janet and Danial. Danial and Janet arrived in time and they went straight into the dining room and were seated at their table and took the menu and ordered dinner Danial Janet and James ordered stakes while Marline ordered fish. During dinner they talked about upcoming wedding where to hold it where to have the reception Danial says to have it in Dublin Because he didn't want to cross the border because he was afraid of the police Marline says she wanted it at home in a church. James says Danial everything up north has changed Liz is gone William is gone and the R.U.C. are gone. Danial nodded his head and said we will see what happens.

They leave the dining room and take seats in the hotel foyer They sit and talk until late until Janet says its ten past twelve it's time we were going Danial asks when the wedding is, Marline says as soon as possible. They all stand up and walk towards the door they stand at the door and give each other and say their goodbyes and agreed to meet again before the wedding. Danial and Janet left the Hotel On their way up to there rooms Marline says to James is it Danial who is getting married or is it us. The two of them laugh. Marline and James give each other a cuddle and a kiss and tell each other that they are in love and go their separate ways to their rooms   Next morning there up early meet up for Breakfast have breakfast, go back to there rooms and pack their bags and carry them down to the lobby. They leave down their bags and go over to the reception to checked out and pay when they check out and go to pay the receptionist says all is paid for Danial had the hotel bill paid in full. As they were leaving Manager meets them at the door shake hands and wishes them luck James says the next hotel we will be staying in will be in California on our honey moon. They thank the manager and say their good byes.   They leave the hotel go to the car park pick up James car and leave for home Marline says I didn't know you came up in the car I thought you came up in the bus the same as me. James says I had to bring the car so as I could keep an eye on you they both laugh. On the way home they talk about the Wedding and agree that as soon as they get home they start working on it and get it arranged.

When they arrived at Marlines house Marline wants James to come in for tea James says he wants to get home as he is very tired and he will callup tomorrow to arrange the wedding. Marline gives James a kiss and say I will see you tomorrow as she leaves the car Marline stands and watches as James drives of down the road. When James car disappears out of sight Marline walks up to the door of her house takes the door keys from her bag and opens the door she lifts some letters lying on the floor closes the door opens a letter stands and reeds it leaves the letters on top of a side board, makes herself a cup of tea and sits down and starts thinking about the wedding as she drinks the tea and falls asleep, when she wakes up the time is five P.M. she jumps up and says to herself I would need to get this house tidied before James comes tomorrow. She starts cleaning and polishing and never stops until it's time to go to bed She goes to bed and as she is so tired she falls asleep immediately. Marline gets up early next morning makes herself tea and toast she gets her notebook and pen as she drinks her tea she writes down all her ideas about the wedding. In no time James car drives into the yard Marline stands up goes to the door opens it and stands at the door and waits for James, when James approaches the door they embrace each other as Marline says come on in. James sits down at the table while Marline makes tea James sits looking at Marline and tells her how much he loves her and how good she looks Marline smiles brings over two cups of tea sets them down on the table gives James a kiss and says I love you.

They drink the tea as they discuss the wedding James says he wants to get married a catholic Marline says she doesn't mind as long as it's in a church then where do we live here or your house. James says my house is too big and I don't want the land and I don't think I would like living here they agreed to buy a new house in town and sell James house and farm and Marlines house they then left and went to see the priest they discussed the wedding with the priest and told him that they were going out Fifty years the priest laughed and said I will make a lovely wedding they planed to get married in two weeks' time.

When they arrive home Marline Phones Janet Next morning Janet and Danial arrive at James house, Danial Tells James he is down to help him with the wedding. The three of them drive up to Marlines house Marline is delighted to see Janet. James and Danial go to look for a hotel while Janet and Marline go looking for clothes to where it wasn't too long until the boys booked a local hotel the hotel Manager ask how many were coming to the wedding James started counting James started counting and says five they met up with the girls that evening and they went to a hotel and talked until late it was only then that Danial and Janet membered that they booked some where to stay and the hotel where they had their meal was fully booked.

It was decided that Danial would spend the night at James house while Janet would stay at Marlines house next Morning Danial and James drove up to Marlines house At about Eleven A.M. Janet and Danial left for home Marline and James went for a drive up to Bundoran and walked Rougie they were so happy marline says we should have went back to see the priest to day and ask him to marry us to morrow all it would have meant was Janet and Danial staying another day James its only ten days until the Saturday and it will all be over.

James says I booked the reception for five guests Marline you should have booked for seven My sister and her husband are coming she is going to give me away James I didn't know, I will phone the hotel tomorrow and let them know.

James visited Marline and brought her a bunch of pink carnations every day while they were getting the house ready for sale On the Wednesday morning James drove up to Marlines at about eleven A.M. parked the car walked up to the front door Marline didn't open the door he tried the door handle the door was locked he walked around to the back door it was locked he stood there wondering where she could be he moved from the back door and looked through the kitchen window, there he saw Marline lying on the kitchen floor. James went back to the door smashed a pane of glass and opened the door ran to Marline when he saw she was very ill he ran to the phone and phoned for an ambulance. He went to Marline got down on his knees took Marline head in his hands Marline says James it's too late James says no as he stroked her hair.

After a short period of time an ambulance arrived with paramedics the paramedics took over from James and started working on Marline. The paramedics lifted Marline onto a stretcher carried her out and put her into the ambulance The paramedic says we are taking Marline to hospital in Enniskillen. The ambulance leaves for Enniskillen with the blue light flashing. James locks up the back door and follows the ambulance to hospital. When James arrives at the hospital he parks the car and goes straight to the emergency department. When he arrives the receptionist informs James that Marline has had a severe hart attack and she has been rushed to theatre for emergency surgency. James sat outside the theatre and prayed After an hour the surgeon comes out and says I am sorry we were too late. James puts his head in his hands and cries. A nurse brings James a cup of tea and says you would need to contact your family James says I have no family. The nurse says what about your wife's family, James she not my wife she is just a friend and as for her family she has a sister Ruby who lives in Omagh I don't know her or where she lives in Omagh. The nurse says we will have to contact the Police to trace Marlines next to kin Two police officers arrive and speak with James.   James told the police officer that marline was a friend Fifty years ago and he lost contact and only met again two week ago and that he didn't know her family. Then James remembered Janet and says she has a friend in Dublin. I have her husband's phone number at home. The police officers says we will drive you home and get the phone number. James says I have my car in the Hospital carpark' The police officer says you are in no state to drive. My will drive your car home and you can go along with him and show him the road and I will follow in the patrol car James agrees. They leave the hospital and go to James car James gives the officer the keys the officer drives James home.   When they arrive at James house James gets Danial's phone number and gives it to the police officer the officer says do you know this man James he is my friend The officer says it would be better if you spoke to him, The police officer go back into James house to use the phone. The officer lifts the phone dials the number and hands the phone to James. Janet answers the phone and James tells her that Marline is dead and that the police were looking for her sister Ruby's phone number to contact her. Janet says I will phone Ruby as I have met her on a few occasions. James says all right phone me as soon as you contact her Janet I will phone you right away. The police officer says we can't leave here until your friend phones back and we are sure that Marline next of kin Is contacted. James you may sit down I am going to make a cup of tea will you like a drink of tea the officer says I would love a cup, James tell your colleague to come in for a cup, the officer goes outside and arrives back with the other officer, One officer sit' s down while the other officer helps James make the tea. James takes a packet of biscuits from a cupboard and opens them the three men sit down drink the tea and eat biscuits. James tells them all about him and Marline until the phone rings.

James answers the phone and says its Janet. Janet speaks to the police officer and tells him that she spoke to Marlines Sister and she is going to look after things She speaks to James and tells him that her and Danial were coming down and that they would be there in about two hours. James hangs up the phone. The police officer says that that we will have to go now James thanks the police officers. The police officer say's that's our job done and thanks James for the tea. James starts to get a bed ready for Danial and Janet coming.

Arrangements are made to bury Marline. Marline is buried on the Saturday the day that she was to get married. After the funeral Janet James Danial Ruby and Ruby's husband went to the hotel and eat the dinner that was to be the wedding dinner. After dinner each went their separate ways. James came home heart broken.

Three weeks later James received a letter from a local solicitor called Nigel to call into his office to discuss Marline's affairs. Next day James made an appointment and called into Nigel's office. Nigel and James shook hands as Nigel says sit down, James takes a seat and sits down Nigel opens a file takes a sealed envelope from the file. Nigel starts to read from the file on the second day of May 20/03 Marline Wilson in this office in this office wrote a private letter and sealed it in my presence left instructions on the event of her death this letter is to be given to James Mc. Williams unopened he hands the letter to James and sys sign here that you received it, James takes the letter and puts it into his coat pocket. Rises to leave when Nigel continues sit down there's more. James sits down again Nigel continues fifteen years Marline came into this office and she was going for hart surgery and she wanted to make a will she says the only family I have is James Mc. Williams, he is my next of kin, she signed a document saying in the event of her death her house and all her worldly possessions were to go to James Mc. Williams including my entire savings.

Nigel says her savings is a considerable sum. James says what will I do with that Nigel it's up to you what to do. James thinks for a minute then instructs Nigel to sell the house and all her belongings. Only her car he wants to keep the car.

My football career

I played football for a local club. When I got the call-up to play for Tyrone, I was delighted. I got to the all-Ireland final against Dublin as a full forward. The first ball came in, I caught it above everyone and made straight for the back of the net, when Cluxton brought me to the ground. The ref throws his arms out and blows for a penalty. Mickey Hart shouts "take that one yourself Michael". I take the ball, set it on the penalty spot. I eye-up Cluxton, step back and take aim. I run forward and give the ball a right kick for the left hand corner of the net. I let out a scream and jump out of bed and discover I had just broken my right foot on the bottom of the bed. That was the start and finish of my football career

Sam and William, by Michael Darcy, 14th November 2018.

When I was a boy in the 1950s there lived in the townland of Tattyreagh, two old brothers named Sam Scot and William Scott. I remember them well. They lived in a beautiful two storey farm house. There was a short avenue in front of the house, about fifty meters long, which led from the front door of the house to the road. At the edge of the road, stood two large sandstone pillars, with two big white gates. Along the left-hand side of the avenue, there grew six nice apple trees, two pear trees and a Victorian plum three. Behind the apple trees there grew six blackcurrant bushes, six gooseberry bushes and four redcurrants. Beside the redcurrants grew some rhubarb and some garlic.

In late summer and autumn; the apples, pears and plumbs were the finest fruit I ever did see. My brothers and I would walk home from school and watch Sam and William gather the lovely fruit and feed it to the pigs, as our mouths watered at the sight of the fruit. To the right-hand side of the avenue lay a lovely mature lawn. There were lovely matured lawns to each side. About one hundred meters further down the road, stood a pair of green gates. They led to the farm yard at the back of the house. As you entered the green gates, to your right hand stood a row of stone farm buildings with a two-storey barn with stone steps leading from the yard up to the barn door. The farmhouse stood to your left, with a back door facing the barn. All animal and farm implements were barred from the front of the house.

Tattyreagh is a small rural village situated five miles from Omagh and three miles from Fintona in County Tyrone. Sam and William came from America back in the 1920's and bought a good arable farm, consisting of about eighty or ninety acres. They kept their farm very tidy and they farmed it extremely well. They had two of the biggest and finest Clydesdale horses I had ever seen. They grew oats, potatoes and barley. They also kept some pigs and milking cows.

Sam and William kept themselves to themselves. Neighbours never had many dealings with the Scott's. People said they would not have any dealings with Sam or William because they were very unlucky, an old neighbour named Bobby Pickering claimed that Sam and William had sold their souls to the devil. Bobby said one evening he went into Sam and William's byre and he saw a big white hare milking the cows. The hare growled at him and he was so scared, he ran for home and was not fit to come out of the house for a week. Bobby said he would never put a foot in a yard or a field belonging to Sam or William again. We walked past Sam and William's house every day, to and from school. In all the days I walked past that house, never once did Sam or William speak to me, which was very unusual because I knew and spoke to every farmer from our house to school and back again.

The Scott brothers started work very early every morning. They worked seven days a week. Back in the 50's nobody worked on a Sunday, and everybody went to church. Sam and William worked every Sunday and never ever entered a church. Every evening on the exact dot of ten minutes to six, the Scott brothers would go into the house and never appear out again until next morning. Every evening on the exact dot of six o'clock the back door of the house would open and out of it would come a big black dog. The dog is as big as an Irish wolfhound and no dog had ever had a shinier coat than this dog had. As the dog comes out of the house, the barn door opens and a man comes out of the barn. He stands at the top of the barn steps. The man has long hair and very long arms. He has the shiniest shoes that any man had ever seen. The dog walks across the yard to the bottom of the barn steps, stands a minute, turns around and walks up the barn steps to the man. When he reached the man he would turn around, face the house and give a big yawn. Then the dog turned around again and entered the barn, followed by the man and the door would close behind them. The dog nor he would be seen again until next evening.

A neighbour man named Walter Tweed lived close by. People used to gather in Tweed's house at night to play cards. One night at the card play, talk came up about the man and the dog in Scott's barn. Old Tweed said he had friends in America and they knew the Scott brothers and that they had done some very bad things. Walter said that the dog should be killed. Everyone at the card play agreed, and Walter said that the dog would have to be shot with silver and it would disappear.

Two young fellas at the card play named Tommy Cork and Joe Lyons decided they would shoot the dog. Tommy and Joe cut up some shillings. They used the silver from the shillings to make two silver bullets. Next evening, they loaded up their gun with a silver bullet and went to the Scott's house. There they wait until Sam and William go into the house. They then took up a position in trees along the road, and waited for the dog. On the dot of six, out comes the dog. Just when the dog is about half way across the yard, Tommy Cork fires the gun. The silver bullet hits the dog. The dog jumps up into the air and turns into a ball of fire. The ball of fire rolls across the yard, up the barn steps into the barn and disappears. The man on the barn steps lets out a roar that was heard miles away and runs into the barn. Neither the dog nor the man was ever seen again. Sam or William never came out of the house for four days. When Sam and William did come out, everything seemed normal until a few days later. Tommy Cork and Joe Lyons went out hunting rabbits. Tommy and Joe never returned home. The police were called, and an inspector Ford arrives and forms a search party. The search party search for five days and Tommy and Joe could not be found anywhere. Inspector Ford calls in a full regiment of the B Specials. After another four days, everyone was exhausted. It was now eleven days since Tommy and Joe had went missing, and not a trace of them could be found. Next day, Inspector Ford called the searchers to organise the days search. Walter Tweed says everywhere has been searched two or three times, except for Scott's yard and barn. Inspector Ford asked why Scott's was not searched. Tweed informs the Inspector about the dog, and that everyone was afraid of the Scott's. The Inspector says "Everyone go home, and I will search Scott's myself".

Inspector Ford arrives at Scott's front door, along with a Sergeant by the name of Reed and a constable by the name of Finn. Sergeant Reed knocks the front door. He gets no reply. He knocks louder. A second time he gets no reply. The Inspector goes around to the back door and knocks loudly and gets no reply. The Inspector says, "Things don't look right here, we will have to go and get permission to break down the door and search the house". They turn away and move towards the green gates, when Constable Finn says, "I am after seeing a strange looking woman go into the barn". They turn back towards the barn. Inspector Ford climbs up the barn steps, followed by Constable Finn. Sergeant Reed stands close to the bottom of the steps. Inspector Ford reaches the top of the steps and he gently opens the door. As he enters the barn, he finds William Scott sitting on a chair, reading from a big book. Inspector Ford goes over to William and grabs the book from William. He flicks through the pages of the book and bangs the book closed. Inspector Ford says to William, "I am taking this book and I am going to burn it". "Now" he says, "William, you have twenty-four hours, to find Tommy Cork and Joe Lyons, or I will be back and arrest both you and Sam and charge you both with their disappearance".

Inspector Ford leaves the barn and calls off the search until next morning, because it had become too dark. Next morning, Inspector Ford arrives back with a search warrant and ten police officers. On his arrival, he has been informed by Walter Tweed, that Tommy and Joe had been found wandering around one of Scott's fields. When interviewed by Inspector Ford, Tommy and Joe said they had been walking around the field for days and could not find a gate to get out of the field. Inspector Ford knocks the back door of the house. Sam Scott opened the door and allowed the police to search the house. The search of the house revealed nothing. The police officers leave the house and proceed to the barn. During a search of the barn nothing is found. Six days later the Scott's barn caught fire and was burnt to the ground.

Tommy Cork and Joe Lyons suffered from bad health for the rest of their lives. They never went hunting again, or told anyone what happened. As for Sam and William, bad luck set in. Their horses died and their cows died. Their crops failed. Nothing would go right for Sam and William. Sam and William sold up, and moved away. Nobody knows where they went. It is believed they moved to Scotland. A man of the name of George Pet and his son James Pet bought the Scott farm and moved into the Scott house. On the first night in the house, George slept in the back bedroom and James slept in a front bed room. On the exact stroke of midnight, the front gate opened and closed again as if someone had come in through it. One minute later, the front door opens and closes again. Then the door to James' bedroom opens and closes again. James is lying sleeping in bed. Something grabs James and throws him on to the floor. James would not enter that bed room again. Every night at twelve o'clock, the front gate opened and closed. The front door opened and closed. The front bedroom door opened and closed.

When George Pet heard about the dog, he and James moved out of the house and into a mobile home. After six months, George Pet finds a sorcery and brings him to the house. The sorcery prays for two days. On the second day, he waits until after twelve twelve o clock. The sorcery opens the bedroom door. He looks into the bedroom. He closes the door again and says, "I am going to have to go in, there's a big black dog in the bed". He says, "this will be a big fight". Next the sorcery says, "everyone stay well back, because when this dog finds he is beat, he will try and bring in some of you to help him."

The sorcery enters the bedroom, taking with him a bottle and a book. After a short while, the noise starts inside the bed room. There was a loud bang from the bedroom and the battle had begun. All night long the fight continued, furniture moved and smashed against the walls, until day light when everything quietened. A short time later the sorcery comes out with the dog inside the bottle and the bottle corked and sealed. George Pet, James Pet and the sorcery take the bottle with the dog inside to the rest point on the farm. On the instructions of the sorcery, they dig a hole and bury the bottle as deep as they could. That was the end of the dog. After that, no one would sleep in the house. The Pet's raised the house to the ground and built a new house. The new house is the worst looking house you ever laid eyes on. The Pets move into the house and everything settled down to normal.

The Car

I was looking for a used diesel family car. Something not too old with low mileage. I wasn't in too big a hurry to buy. I searched garages near and far looked at dozens of cars of all makes. I could not find the car I was looking for. One Wednesday morning in the middle of July, my wife and I decided we would travel down to see some friends in county Antrim. Just as we were leaving home, at about ten o clock in the morning, there was a very heavy shower of rain. As we drove along, the rain bounced off the road. The sun was shining and you could see little rainbows rising from the road. Eventually the rain stopped. As the sun shone, the steam rose from the tarmac in clouds. It was beautiful

We stopped in Cookstown, had a very nice cup of tea and did some window shopping. When we returned to our old Vauxhall car, it was so hot you could have fried an egg on the roof. We got into the car and continued our journey towards Antrim. The sun shone so strong and the car was so hot, I was starting to regret making the journey. I stopped at a petrol station to buy a bottle of water.

As I got out of the car I saw this lovely blue Renault car for sale. I went over to the car for a closer look. It was a Renault Laguna 1.9 diesel car. The closer I got to the car the better it looked. As I examined the car, it looked perfect. I went into the garage to enquire about the Renault car for sale. I was met by a very forceful salesman, who told me the car was one year old with 11,000 miles and had one lady owner from new. The owner had been a doctor. After another inspection and a test drive, I decided this was the car I was looking for and that I would buy it. I talked to the salesman again. We agreed a reasonable price and I bought the car.

Two days later, my brother drove me the thirty five miles to pick up the Renault car at the garage. We arrived at the garage at eleven o'clock and inspected the Renault again. My brother, on examining the car, says to me "There is something wrong with that car. It's too cheap and that salesman, I do not like him. There is something fishy about him. He wants to sell that car but he isn't going near it". I did not listen to my brother. All I could think of was this nice blue Renault. I was very pleased with the car. I left my brother and went into the garage office. As I entered the office, the salesman rose from his chair and we shook hands. He offered me a seat and reassured me about the Renault. He did the paper work, I handed over the money and he walked me to the Renault.

The sales man handed me the keys. As I reached for the keys, a blond haired woman appeared beside us, snatched the keys from my hand and threw them to the ground. I stood there in disbelief as the sales man picked up the keys. He apologised for the woman who had disappeared. I noticed that the salesman's demeanour had changed completely. I got into the car and started it. As I closed the door, the salesman said his goodbye's and walks back towards the office. I drove my Renault slowly across the forecourt and out onto the road. I headed for home as proud as a peacock with my new blue Renault. I arrived home at about half past three, parked the car in front of my house. I went into the kitchen and joined the wife in a nice cup of tea and talked about the nice new blue Renault.

Sometime later, I went out to take my wife for a drive in my new car could not believe what I was seeing. My nice new blue Renault had rolled backwards down the driveway and smashed into the gatepost. As I ran down the driveway towards the car, I saw the blond haired woman jump from the car. When I arrived at the car I could see no one.

I informed my local garage, who came and towed my car away to be repaired. Two weeks later, I got my new blue Renault back. It had been repaired perfectly and it cost me six hundred pounds. When I went to collect the car the mechanic asked me "Who was the woman who came into the garage every day and inspected the car?"

Two weeks later I went to my local sports day, parked my Renault in the car park. I enjoyed a great day and on returning to my Renault I found that a horse and gig had ran-a-mock in the carpark and had ran into my Renault. I was back to the garage and paid four hundred pounds for repairs. Two weeks later I travelled to a football match, parked my Renault in the carpark and returned to find my lovely blue Renault had been hit with a ball. I was back to the garage again for one hundred and fifty pounds of repairs. One week later I left home to go to a neighbour's funeral, half mile down the road. The time belt on the car broke, so I was back to the garage with my nice blue Renault. This time the repairs cost me six hundred pounds. The mechanic says "I never have seen a car as unlucky as that Renault".

In all the time I owned the Renault, it refused to go to a funeral. Every time I decided to go to a funeral, the Renault had a major breakdown. The year and a half I owned the Renault, it was involved in eighteen accidents, every single one happened when it was parked. The final straw was when I visited a neighbour's house on some business. I parked the Renault in the neighbour's yard, walked forty meters to his office. I went into the office to discuss business. Ten minutes later we heard a loud bang. We went out to investigate. My blue Renault was gone. It had rolled backwards down the driveway, over the ditch and down thirty meters into an embankment. It was a complete write-off. My neighbour drove me home, and not long after that, a police officer arrived at my door looking for the owner of the blue Renault. I brought him inside and asked him what he wanted. He asked me who was driving the Renault when it rolled down the embankment. I told him there was no one in the car. He then said they had got several reports of a blond haired woman trapped in the blue Renault at the bottom of the embankment. The emergency services responded, and they could not find the woman. I told him this woman was seen before and that she was a ghost. He wrote all I said into his note book and left. He did not believe one word I said. I had the blue Renault lifted out of the Glen and taken to the scrapyard and I bought myself a nice new white Vauxhall. I thought that was the end of my nice new blue Renault.

The scrap dealer told me some time later that he had regretted ever seeing my Renault. It had cost him a small fortune. Since the time that blue Renault came into his yard there is a ghost in the yard. A blond woman has been seen walking around the yard on several occasions, and seems to be looking for something in his yard. I told him I had regretted ever seeing the Renault, because it had cost me a fortune and had been nothing but bother. I decided I would investigate the previous owner of the blue Renault, as I had the name and address. I travelled to the address and found a derelict house. I saw a blond woman looking out of a window at me. When I went to speak to her she disappeared. The place felt creepy so I left. As I came out onto the road, I met a man who asked me what I was doing at Doctor Weir's house. He wasn't too pleased when I told I was looking for the doctor who lived here. He asks me what I wanted to see her for. I told him it was private, between me and her. He got very annoyed and said that I wasn't to move as he was calling the police.

A police car arrived with and two uniformed police officers got out of the car. One went over and spoke to the man for a short while. After that, he went and spoke to the other officer. They then came over to me. The officer asked me my name and my address and what I was doing there. As I tried to explain, he wrote everything down. The other officer catches me by the arm and says "you will have to come with us". He walked me over to the car and put me into the back of the car and closed the door. The two officers get into the front seats and drive off with me in the back. I look round the back of the car. There was a screen between the front of the car and the back. There were no door handles on the inside of the back doors. There were no words spoken until I light a cigarette. The officer in the front passenger seat turned around and roared at me "you don't smoke in my car!" At that, he opened his door and held it open. Only then I noticed that the windows did not open. I smiled to myself that the smoke was annoying him because he was not a very nice person.

We arrived at the police station. The Officer got out of the car, opened the back door, took me by the arm and led me inside. When inside, he took me to a cell, put me inside and closed the door. Sometime later, another officer opened the door and said "come with me". He took me to another room. As I enter the room, he closes the door and disappeared. In all my life I had never seen a room like this. No window and just one bare lightbulb in the ceiling, one table, three chairs and the door. I sat down on the chair next to the door. Just as I sat down, the door opened and in came two men. Each had a bundle of papers under their arm. One had black hair and the other had grey hair. The one with the black, hair hit the leg of the chair I was sitting on a kick, with his boot. He says "you don't sit on my chair, you sit behind the table". I rose and went and sat behind the table. The two men sat down in front of the table facing me. The grey haired man introduced himself and the other man as detectives. He then asked me my name. When I told him my name, he started reading from a sheet of paper "I am arresting you and anything you say will be written down and will be used in evidence against you. I am questioning you about the murder of Doctor Weir". Only then I realised this was serious. I sat there like a trapped rat.

The only way out of this room was through the door that had no handle on the inside and past the two men sitting between me and the door. The two men fired questions at me one after the other. "You were here, you were there, you did this and you did that; you murdered so and so, you drove the car, you know the salesman, you and he are friends….." I tried to tell them that I only bought a car that I wished I had never seen. It seemed to me that no matter what I said they seemed to never listen. They twisted everything I said. They seemed to have their own agenda and were convinced I murdered this woman. After what seemed like forever, they both closed their files and left the room. Two minutes later, the grey haired man returned, and says to me "you are free to go".

The detective walked me to the station door and I asked him what was going on. He told me that the Doctor had been found dead in her car and her death was believed to be suicide. The salesman I bought the car from owned the garage and he was the Doctor's boyfriend. They suspected that it wasn't suicide and that he murdered her. "That was over three years ago, and you turned up asking about her. We thought you knew something and we had to satisfy ourselves that you knew nothing. The man you spoke to was the Doctor's brother. He phoned us immediately and we had to take you in for questioning". I said I understood why they had to question me and asked "will you leave me back to my car?" The detective says "your car is here, we will bring it round to you in a minute." Just as he spoke, my car came around the corner with a uniformed officer driving it. As the uniformed officer disembarked from my car I asked "what right have you to drive my car!" The detective says "we had to bring in your car to be searched".

I got into my car and headed for home thinking the live ghost is worse than the dead one.

The Corn Stacks

Through the forties and fifties, in the townland of Annawhisker, in the county of Tyrone, there lived a well to do farmer by the name of Robert Dunlop. Robert lived in a big two-story house. It was believed to be the nicest house in the County of Tyrone. Everyone talked about the lovely marble floors in the house and the marble here and there through the house. I never saw any of the marble until after the house was burnt. Robert farmed a farm of very rich soil, which consisted one hundred and ninety acres. Robert Dunlop insisted everyone addressed him as Mr. Dunlop. Robert was a man who believed that time was money. He was the sort of man who believed that if you stopped to eat you were wasting time. Robert's religion was money - he used to say that he didn't care where the money came from as long as it came to him.

Robert came to Annawhisker from America. It is believed Robert and his father were involved in the American civil war and were involved in some very bad actions. It is also believed they were involved with the KKK. they came to Ireland to avoid the authority's catching up with them.

Robert lived a long life. His wife died at a young age, and they had no family. I did not know his wife, she had died before my time.

What he lacked in family, he made up for in corn. Growing corn was arduous work. First, you had to plough the ground to make it ready, sow the corn, wait tirelessly for it to grow and ripen. When it ripened in the harvest time it had to be mowed, gathered by hand, and tied into bundles called sheaths. The sheths were then stood in bundles of four to dry. These were called stooks. Four sheafs to the stook. After three weeks, the stooks were gathered and built into what were called lumps. One hundred stooks made one lump. When the corn was dry the lumps were gathered and built into stacks. Ten lumps made one stack. Four sheafs made one stook. One hundred stooks to the lump. Ten lumps to the stack. The stacks were covered with rushes to keep them dry over the winter. In the spring time the thrasher mill would come and separate the seed corn from the straw. Then, the whole cycle would be repeated.

Annawhisker was sparsely populated back then, and Roberts closest neighbours were a large family by the name of McMahon. George McMahon and his wife Janice, who unlike Mr. Dunlop had plenty of children. None of them, at this stage, were yet married, and all lived at home. The eldest girls, Nora and Lizzie worked in the local hospital. The boys, all six of them - John, Jim, William, Michael, Thomas and Peter, worked on the farm. Margaret, the youngest of the lot, helped to look after the homestead. The McMahons loved hunting and kept four hounds suited to the job. They were fierce animals when a hare was involved, ferocious at the sight of deer, but tame and placid around the children. They made easy the demands of their job, doubled as guard dogs in days before they were much needed, and provided unwavering companionship to the McMahons. The esteem in which the McMahons held their dogs carried over to all those about them. Although George McMahon had no love of Mr. Dunlop, he was nothing if not a good neighbour and insisted the same of his family. George Mc Mahon had a belief that if a man is not a gentleman; let him see *you are* a gentleman.

Once their own work and chores were finished, the McMahon girls would call in on Mr. Dunlop and make sure his house was in order. The boys would work the corn without complaint. They were satisfied simply because it was too much for one old man, and they never asked anything in return. They whiled away their autumn evenings on Mr Dunlop's farm, long hours after finishing the work on their own. They enjoyed the long warm evenings, the strain of the work, and each other's company. It was on such an evening with the boys in the fields, and little craic in the house, that Nora and Margaret took it upon themselves to tidy Mr. Dunlop's house. Knowing the task would be made the better with their brother's eventual break to the kitchen for tea.

Almost upon leaving the house, their want for company was met in the form of Donal McFee, shooing a lone calf in front of him. McFee, much like his neighbours, kept a small farm a mile up the road. Unlike George McMahon, he had few sons to keep the place. His fences and hedges were often in a sorry state. When George McMahon took his evenings for some well-earned rest, and Mr. Dunlop added to his fortune with the help of the McMahon boys, Donal McFee often spent his evenings traipsing the roads in search of rogue cattle, that had set out in search of greener pastures. On seeing this all too familiar sight, the girls laughed at McFee's luck in finding his escapee before dark. Says he, "Ah, sure all the luck on this road will be on you two girls. You're off to Mr. Dunlop's, no doubt, and when he pushes his feet up, the whole lot will go to you. The farm, the house, and the millions he has hidden away in it! You'll be fit to buy the whole of Annawhisker, my lot included, and let me get a bit of damn peace from these cattle."

Says Nora, "Mr. Dunlop would sooner buy a gold coffin and a diamond headstone so he could take it all with him than leave it to the likes of us!". Says he, "Ha-ha, sure what you earn here will be paid for in a heavy price". Before he could finish his thought, the calf had made another bolt for freedom, maybe sensing that his driver was distracted. McFee took off after it, no doubt relieved in some way that it was at least running towards home. The girls had often taken cows to be stupid animals, but as they laughed at the calf's antics, they wondered if calves were smarter than they believed and maybe they only became stupid as they grew up, much like they suspected of adults. Or perhaps it was just that the stupidest always find a way to come out on top.

Once McFee was out of sight, the girls picked up the conversation the calf had railroaded. Says Margaret, "It would be nice if Old Mr Dunlop did leave us a few bob. Not all of it, mind, but enough to buy a house in the town and maybe get married". Says Nora, "Just don't be waiting on it, that one will live forever." Says Margaret, "I saw the grave digger wagging the spade at him, telling him he's ready!" Says Nora, "That wasn't a spade he was waving, that was the white flag, he's given up on waiting on him!" They would never talk with such disrespect in either their own home, nor in Mr. Dunlop's, but on this small stretch of road they allowed themselves to relax and make each other laugh. They both knew full well that there was no harm in their words. He may have been old, but Mr. Dunlop was as healthy as a wild duck, and they knew it.

When they got to Mr. Dunlop's house, they found him sitting in the living room, his face the colour of yesterday's fire, and his breath like the bellows. Throwing an arm each under him, they dragged him upstairs in silence, the guilt of their jokes falling off them. Once they had him in his bed, Nora raced to fetch Dr McGinn, grabbing Mr. Dunlop's old bicycle on the way out. She nearly broke her front teeth trying to get her leg over the cross bar. Margaret spent her time tending to the sick man, making him as comfortable as she could in the hope of alleviating the weight of her earlier comments. Dr McGinn arrived in due course, and befitting a man of his stature, spoke to the girls with not an ounce of emotion in his voice. Says he, "You've done the right work here girls, but Mr. Dunlop shall be dead by morning. Go on home now, you're of no use to him".

Shaken, but no less relived at the doctor's absolution, the girls gathered their brothers from the field, and the eight of them set for home to tell their parents. On hearing the news, George McMahon declared that it isn't right for any man to die alone, but as kindly a neighbour as he is, he had no wish to spend his evening with the dying Mr. Dunlop. So it was decided that that Michael and Thomas would hold vigil. The two solid sons did not want to have anything to do with it, but they feared shirking their duties both to their father and as men themselves, and so they set off in the dark to watch a man die.

The black night on the walk was more than enough for them, and as soon as the entered the house, they set about lighting every lamp they could find. Once they had the downstairs glowing like a summer afternoon, they took a lamp each and headed upstairs, and set about the same task. They had lit the entire house, so that someone in the distance might think it ablaze, save for Mr. Dunlop's room itself. Finding no more distractions to keep them from it, they opened the door and found him much as their sisters had described. Realising that there was less to fear of this old man now on this autumn night with him in his room, than there was during the autumn evenings with him in his fields, they soon made themselves comfortable and got to chatting, enjoying the rarity of late night company. Talk of corn stacks made way for talk of girls, and just as Michael was ready for the first time to let his brother in on his designs for marriage, Mr. Dunlop stirred in his bed, and began to toss and turn, moaning from the depth of his lungs. With no ideas on how else to ease his suffering, Michael went to the kitchen to fetch a glass of water, not considering how the unconscious man would go about drinking it. While searching for a clean glass, for the girls had never managed to get to their task of cleaning the house, Michael heard an unearthly roar from his brother, the kind of noise the hounds would make when they set off after a hare, and like the hounds, Michael bounded out of the kitchen to set his teeth into whatever had tested his brother.

Says Michael, "What happened?". Thomas was starting to turn the same colour as Mr. Dunlop, who had since quietened down. Says Thomas, "Thon chair you were sitting on is after sliding across the floor on its own, and something fired me from off mine!" Says Michael "Now, it's bad enough that we're set up in here with himself, don't you be going adding ghost stories to it!" As he said this, Michael saw the colour, or the lack of it, on his brother's face, and the film of sweat on his brow. Before he had a chance to come to a conclusion, he felt an almighty force on his chest. He told me since that his first thought was that his brother had pushed him, continuing his prank for want of sleep, but when his brain caught up with his senses, he realised that his brother was tumbling out the door alongside him, and the only other man who could have pushed him was the dying Mr. Dunlop, still on his bed, with no more strength than an infant in any case.

Saying nothing, but with the fear running through them, the two boys braced themselves and made for the sick room, ready to confront whatever had just pushed them, but the moment Michael's foot came near the threshold, the door swung shut in his face and was bolted from the inside. That was enough for their bravery and they made a run for the front door, only to find it locked solid and the bolt unmovable. Already knowing what they would find, they went for the backdoor, and confirmed that they were locked in. In a fearful fit of desperation, Thomas threw a kitchen chair at the big window that looked out over the corn fields, and the chair bounced back to his feet. The chair had no more effect on the glass than throwing water would have.

Says Michael, "It's all right, the sun will be up in a couple of hours- we'll just bunk down here for the night". He already knew how pointless his reassurances were before he spoke them, but they were made worse the moment he finished speaking. A crash came from upstairs, like a man being thrown over a table. The boys had seen a few fights in the pub over the years, when farmers battered each other over owed favours, or hammered each other's sons over daughters led astray, but they had never heard a noise like what was going on in the room above them. They imagined the three biggest men they had ever witnessed, wrestling to the death, and using every stick of furniture as a weapon. What little had remained of their bravery vanished, and they barricaded themselves into the kitchen- pushing first the dresser against the door, then the table and the kitchen chairs behind that. Michael picked up a blunt axe that Mr. Dunlop had beside the door, perhaps intending to sharpen it, and Thomas took the poker form the fire. They pushed themselves back against the wall, and sat, staring at their makeshift defences, not able to talk over the crashing and roaring form above them. As the first sliver of sunlight cracked through the big kitchen window, the noise stopped as quickly as it had started, and was quickly followed by the banging of the doors being thrown open, a cool breeze flowing through the kitchen door bringing the boys to their senses. If Annawhisker had an Olympic committee, the two boys would have been signed up that morning for every race, for no-one had ever made quicker time along that road.

George McMahon, pragmatic as always, on hearing the frightened and confused ramblings of his sons, quietly sent them to bed and gave the other boys tasks. John set off on his bicycle to fetch the Sargent, and Peter headed to inform select neighbours. George was rounding up the posse. When all were assembled - George, John, Peter, Sergeant Weir the Sheriff and three who shall remain nameless; they made their way to Mr. Dunlop's house to begin their investigation. Just as the boys had found Mr. Dunlop as the girls had said, so now the men found Mr. Dunlop's house as the boys had said. The front and back doors were wide open, and the kitchen was barricaded from the inside. Instructing the rest to wait outside, Sargent Weir and George McMahon went in search of Mr. Dunlop.

The room was destroyed. Pieces of furniture were shattered and strewn about the floor. The curtains and clothes from the demolished wardrobe were torn and scattered about the place. The bed had collapsed, but upon it, Mr. Dunlop seemed unharmed, although obviously dead. He had not a mark on him, but his grey face and blue lips betrayed his state. Clutched tightly in his rigor mortis grip was a red book with a black spine. Sargent Weir pulled it from him, with no small amount of effort, and opened it at random. The blood ran from his face, leaving him a colour that was now all to common in this room. Much to his relief, Dr Mc Ginn entered the room, saving him from having to describe what he had read. The doctor officially pronounced Mr. Dunlop's passing, and suggested that any damage to the room must have taken place in his absence and had no effect on the corpse. This, along with the extent of the destruction, was enough to convince the Sargent that the McMahon boys had played no part in the old man's death, and he set affairs in motion. The funeral was planned for the following morning.

There was a strange air about the funeral procession. The usual mourning had made way for a sense of unease, and rumours had spread like gorse fire about Annawhisker. Neither Thomas nor Michael had spoken much since the morning before, but these things have their own way of getting about; stories carried on the wind. This odd feeling had obviously spread to the animals, who stirred restlessly when the coffin was put on the trap, but they followed commands and began moving along the road. It was only as we came upon the corn stacks that the horses really began making trouble, but instead of rearing up or kicking, they stopped in the middle of road, and refused to move. The horses as one dropped their heads, and no amount of coaxing could persuade them to move a muscle. Everyone around grew agitated, and the whispers got up about what was causing the horses behaviour, or lack of it.

Says George, "From the day and hour he arrived in Annawhisker, Dunlop caused nothing but trouble, and he's still causing trouble as he's leaving it". It was and still is, the most damning thing I had ever heard George McMahon say. He rallied a few men around him, and they put the coffin upon their shoulders, carrying it past the corn stacks, eyes fixed ahead. The moment they were clear of them, the horses followed along behind, and the men put the coffin back in its place. The funeral was otherwise unexceptional. Mr Dunlop was put in the ground, and everyone tried to forget the whole thing. Some had more success than others.

Not two weeks after the funeral, late in the afternoon, Thomas and Michael took the hounds and set out for the hunt, hoping to get their minds back on their own affairs. Having little success, they turned for home, the sun setting behind them. Their brief chatter dropped to silence when they came as far as the corn stacks, both boys lost in their own thoughts. Neither could look in the direction of the stacks, behind which lay that house. They focused on their fee, imagining the place not to be there. It was only as the dogs kicked up a racket that they looked up, first to the dogs running mad in fear. Then to old Mr. Dunlop standing by the corn stacks, glaring down upon them, with the same ashen skin as the last time they saw him alive.

The dogs arrived home before the boys. The four of them were in a frenzied state. When Margaret tried to calm them down, these four pups she had helped rear as a child herself, they lashed at her, teeth bare and saliva drooling from the blood red lips. Faring rabies, George McMahon, with a weight in his heart but no choice in his head, reached for the shotgun. With the dogs still lying bleeding on the street, and Margaret wailing in the kitchen, George gathered his other boys and went in search of Michael and Thomas. He found them, in the woods nearby, sullen and unresponsive, and transfixed on nothing as the horses at the funeral. George and his four other sons struggled to carry them home. When they came close to the house, he cried a desperate call for help. In all of their years together, Janice had never before heard her husband's voice break. Together as a family, nine carrying, and two being carried, they made it into the house. Thomas and Michael were put to bed, and Dr McGinn made his third visit to Annawhisker in two short weeks. His speech was much the same as his first visit. The two McMahon boys died from shock during the night.

When Sergeant Weir heard about the McMahon boys he too returned to Annawhisker, but this time he took with him a clergyman. The two spoke to George for a long while. The sun set outside the kitchen window, and when it rose again, the three were still huddled around the kitchen table. At that time, George sent out his remaining boys - John, Jim, William and Peter - to pass a message to every house in Annawhisker. By breakfast time, over thirty neighbours had gathered. Saying nothing to the crowd, Sargent Weir went to his bicycle and pulled from his satchel the same red book with the black spine that Mr. Dunlop had clutched to his chest in his death throes. He looked at it gravely and put it in his pocket. He called four stout men to him and sent them on an errand.

The troop set off, with the clergyman leading the charge, his bible open, and the only noise to be heard were the verses he recited at the top of his lungs. Behind him, was Sargent Weir, the other book, the bible's counterpart, tucked securely in the crook of his arm. When they reached the corn stacks, the clergy man read for what seemed an eternity, his voice dropping to a low rumble, then rising and booming again. No one else spoke. Eventually, he stopped, and beckoned George McMahon. George stepped forward, and producing a cigarette lighter from his pocket, set to lighting each and every corn stack. Every lump. Every stook. Every sheaf. The flames crackled through the hard autumn work of the dead McMahon boys. The clergyman prayed over the pyres.

As the fires reached their height, the clergyman turned and began walking toward the house, once again reading aloud from The Bible. Almost as if it was rehearsed, Sargent Weir held the red book with the black spine out in front of him, and set off after the priest, with George McMahon behind him. Followed by what seemed to be the entirety of the Annawhisker community, some seventy people. As they made their way from the heat of the corn fires and closer to the house, the Sargent and the Priest began to perspire heavily. The priest looked unsteady on his feet, and someone stepped forward to give him support, let he collapse to the ground. When they had reached the house, they found Sargent Weir's four helpers finishing the task of dousing the house in oil. George McMahon sparked his lighter again and waiting for Sargent Weir to toss the book in through the door, threw his lighter after it. They watched for a moment to see the flame catch the oil and then the book, and pulled the door closed.

The crowd moved away from the house, and still no one speaks. After ten minutes, the house starts to creek. By this stage, the Priest, still reading from his bible, is so overcome that he had to sit down. The people gathered around flicking their eyes between him and the house. Sargent Weir and George McMahon stood closest to the house, eyes fixed upon the door, almost as if keeping guard lest someone, or something, escape. Suddenly, the house explodes into flames, throwing the crowd back with it. It is only now that the Sargent and George seem able to put some distance between themselves and the house. The flames reach fifty meters into the sky with the sparks reaching one hundred metres. It's the most spectacular fireworks display ever visited upon Annawhisker. It is quickly followed by the most deafening, harrowing noise ever visited upon Annawhisker. There rose a screeching as if hundreds of people were still in the house, but bellowing, rising defyingly above the cracks of the timber burning. The people there ran in fear for their own homes, barricading their own doors, to keep them from what they knew not. The only people remaining at the burning house, bracing themselves against the deafening, unearthly noise was Sargent Weir, The Priest, and the remnants of the McMahon family. The noise kept up for over an hour, the roaring and screeching echoing around the hills. When the noise finally stopped there was an eerie silence hung about. Even the flames, still licking at the timber frame of the house, fell silent.

Says the Priest, "That's the end of old Mr Dunlop and his friends". The fire eventually subsided, and three days later, a lawyer arrived at the McMahon house. The remaining McMahon family gathered about him in the kitchen. Mr. Dunlop had divided all his worldly good three ways, to be distributed on the event of his death. His fortune was to go solely to Margaret. The land was to be divided between Peter and William. Margaret immediately set off on her bicycle to inform the Priest that she wanted nothing to do with the money, and that he was to take the money and donate it to wherever he saw best fit. They made several failed attempts to pass on the land. No-one in Annawhisker, nor anywhere surrounding it, wanted to set foot upon those fields let alone farm them. So they gave the land to the Ministry of Agriculture who planted the entire land with trees. When a contractor was sent to clear the rubble from the house, they lifted the lovely large marble tiles from the kitchen floor, only to discover RIP carved into one of the tiles. On closer inspection it was discovered that the marble tiles were headstones stolen from grave yards scattered all over the whole county. I never did find out about the contents of that book with the red cover and the black spine, and to this day, I am glad of it. People say that the sergeant says there was a devil in every page.

The Cow

It was a lovely autumn evening and the sun was setting. I had just finished my chores when my friend Frank arrived. He says "We will go to McMulkins to watch a film". Joe McMulkin was, I believe, from Dungannon. He would come every year and erect a big tent in a field along the main road between Omagh and Fintona, and show films every night. It was only about half a mile from our house.

Remember this was back in 1958, so we had no television. Frank and myself decided we would cycle. It was lovely cycling down the road with leaves dropping off the trees along one side of the road. There were about six damson plum trees growing there. We stopped to eat some damsons and then we cycled to the shop. At the shop we bought three penny dainties each, to eat during the film. When we arrived at the field the first thing we saw was McMulkins car. It was sitting in front of the tent, and it was the biggest car I had ever seen. It was a big giant American limo. We paid two shillings each to get in to see the film. In today's money two shillings is about ten pence.

When we entered the tent, it was almost full of people. We found two seats on the left hand side near the back of the tent. The film was just about to start. It was a Tarzan film and we thought it was brilliant. When the film was over we made out way out of the tent and into the field. On our way out of the field everyone was talking about the film and McMulkins big car. One old neighbour woman called Cassie said "McMulkin must be very rich to own a big car like that". Another neighbour named Mickey said "He's not rich, if he was rich he would buy Tarzan a pair of trousers and not have him running around half naked". An argument got up about the film and Tarzan's clothes. More people got involved. At one stage we thought they were going to go and buy clothes for Tarzan. After listening to them for a while we picked up our bicycles.

We headed for home it was very dark. We cycled along the road talking and laughing about the film and how stupid the old people were thinking that Tarzan was a real man. We came to a part of the road known as the turn, and just as we rounded the turn this big black monster appeared in front of me. I cycled straight into it and fell off my bicycle. The monster let out a loud roar and I jumped into the air. I was so scared. I jumped up and left my bicycle lying on the road and ran for home as fast as I could run. When I arrived home, Frank was already there, and he had told the story about the monster. He told them the monster had got me but he had got away. Daddy and my brother fetched a lamp and went to search for the monster. On arriving at the turn on the road they found my bicycle but no monster. Frank was so scared my daddy had to walk him home. I could hardly sleep that night I was so scared. Ext morning when my father was on his way to work he found the monster. The monster turned out to be a neighbour's old black cow that was standing on the road. I had cycled straight into it.

The Crock Fairy Fort

Around where we lived in the townland of Tattyreagh , in the north of Ireland, there are several ring forts known as Fairy Forts. A fort consists of about half an acre of good arable land. All forts are built in a circle, with a white thorn hedge. Some have a mote outside the hedge. They are all placed on the top of a hill or high ground. When you stand in a fort and look around, you can see six more forts. It is believed that the fairies still live in some forts. When you enter them you can feel you are being watched.

When I decided to write this story, I went to visit the fort where this story took place. When I entered the fort, I could hear music. I got a very strange feeling as if I was being watched. As I walked around, I was approached by a big fawn coloured Labrador dog. As I walked around the fort, the dog walked backwards in front of me. When I left the fort the dog disappeared. When I got back to my car I had a flat tyre.

So, to continue with this story, in the townland of Tattyreagh there is a round hill known as Crock. Crock consists of around about two hundred acres of arable land. On the top of Crock there is a Fairy Fort with a high white thorn hedge and surrounded by a deep mote. This fort belonged to a man called Charlie Crawford. Charlie was known by the nickname of Grey Charlie. He got this nickname because there are a lot of Crawford's who live in the same local area and Charlies mother's maiden name was Grey. Grey Charlie was known as the local horse doctor. When an animal became sick you would send for grey Charlie who would either cure or kill the animal. Grey Charlie was also a very good famer. Charlie was married with no family. His wife died very young. Charlie told a story about when his wife was very sick, and the doctor sent her to hospital. The hospital sent her home again and said they could do nothing for her and that she needed a kidney transplant. Charlie says he had to do a kidney transplant himself. When I asked where he got the kidney from, he said he used a sheep's kidney.

The Drumconnelly Road runs over Crock from north to south. At the bottom of Crock, on the north side, the Drumconnelly Road is joined by the Old Fort Road. It is said that Saint Patrick travelled along the Old Fort road and when he reached the Drumconnelly Road, he looked left, then looked right, raised his right hand and said "the back of my hand to crock". He then turned left down the Drumconnelly Road. When he arrived in the Townland of Drumconnelly, he met a Knight on a white horse. The knight told him to go no further along that road, as there was a dragon in the Townland of Duna Nigh and it was devouring everything in its path. Saint Patrick asked the Knight for his horse as he himself would fight the dragon. The Knight gave Saint Patrick the horse. When Patrick reached Duna Nigh he was confronted by the dragon. Patrick dismounted from his horse and ordered the horse to fight the Dragon. The horse killed the dragon. It then went crazy and Saint Patrick ordered the horse into the lake. To this very day, every seven years on the seventh day of May, the horse comes out of the lake and runs around the lake seven times and then goes back into the water.

It is believed that it is very unlucky to interfere with a Fairy Fort. Grey Charlie said "that's all superstition, I am going to plough up the Fort and grow potatoes". There came some good weather in the middle of January and Grey Charlie decided he would plough up the Fort at about nine o clock. It was a lovely Monday morning. A mist was clearing over Crock and the rays of sun were breaking through the clouds.

Grey Charlie and a man who worked for Charlie known by the name of John Doak, hitched the horses and headed to plough up the fort. John was a nephew of Grey Charlie. Grey Charlie and John arrived in the Fort. They marked the rigging and started to plough. The rigging is a mark you make with the plough along the top and bottom of the field. This is so that when you are ploughing you know where to start and finish, to keep your ploughing in a straight line. They started ploughing the Fort and everything went well for about two hours. Then one of Charlie's horses stumbled on the rigging and broke his leg and had to be put down. That was the ploughing finished for the day. John said "that's the curse of the Fort". Charlie said "a horse could break a leg in any field".

The next day Charlie and John started ploughing again. Charlie left the gate open and the cows came into the Fort. When John and Charlie were removing the cows from the Fort, two cows fell into the mote. It took every man in the Townland to get the cows out of the mote. When Charlie entered the cow shed the next morning, he found one of his cows had died during the night. It took the whole day to bury the cow. Charlie said to John to hitch the horses so they could go ploughing. John said "I will hitch the horses, but I am not going to plough that Fort". Charlie said, "hitch the horses and I will plough the Fort myself". John did as he was asked and Charlie set off to the fort. He never stopped ploughing all day. By night time Charlie had most of the Fort ploughed. He arrived home, pleased with his day's work.

On entering the cow shed the next morning, Charlie founds two cows dead. John said "that's the curse of the Fort". Charlie said "that's superstition. The cows must have eaten something that poisoned them". Then Charlie said "you bury the cows and I will finish ploughing the Fort". John got some neighbours to help him bury the cows, while Charlie set off to finish ploughing the fort. That evening, Charlie did not return home. When it was getting late, John decided he would go and look for Charlie. When he arrived at the Fort, it was full of lights, like candles. There was a strange noise coming from the Fort. It sounded as if there were many children crying. John was so scared he was afraid to enter the Fort to look for Charlie. Some neighbours arrived to investigate as they had seen the lights. John informed them that Charlie was missing. They decided they would have to go into the Fort and look for Charlie. On entering the fort, the lights disappeared, but the crying sound continued. They found Charlie lying on the ground with two broken legs. Charlie told them that the horse stumbled and fell on top of him. Charlie was brought to hospital where he died four days later. Every night the fort was full of lights and the crying continued day and night. Nobody would go near the fort.

After Grey Charlie's funeral, John Doak inherited Grey Charlie's farm. John decided he would have to turn back the ploughing. On a Tuesday morning John went up to the fort and started to turn back the ploughing. John worked hard every day. On a cold Thursday evening when John was finishing for the evening, the crying stopped. As he turned over a plough scrape in the fort, there he found an iron bar. The bar was about one meter long by about four centimetres. John carried home the iron bar and stood it at the side of his house. Next morning John goes back to the Fort and starts turning the ploughing. After about two hours John is finished.

He stood up, looked around and congratulated himself on the good job he had done. The Fort looked as if it never had been ploughed. On leaving the Fort for home, John could hear sweet music. That night there were no more lights to be seen in the Fort and everything on Crock settled back to normal

That was until John decided he would repair the plough. He loaded the plough into the cart, along with the iron bar which he had found in the Fort and headed for the blacksmith. On arriving at the blacksmiths, John explained to Jack the blacksmith what he wanted. Jack lifted the iron bar, took it over to the fire, measures it and marked it here and there. He then lifts it and puts it into the fire. When the iron started to heat, John looked at it closely, then grabbed hold of the iron bar. He pulled it out of the fire and ran out the door. He threw the iron bar into the cart. John jumped into the cart, grabbed the horse reins and headed off down the road as fast as the horse and cart could travel. John didn't come back for six days. When he arrived back, he was the richest man in the whole county of Tyrone. John will not tell anybody where he got all the money. It is believed the iron bar John found in the fort was solid gold. Every Saturday night John Doak hitches up the horse and cart and travels to the local pub and gets full drunk. When he is full, the bartender carries John out and puts him into the cart and the horse takes him home. It is strongly believed, that the fairies drive the horse home for John Doak on a Saturday night. When John wakes up on Sunday mornings, he finds that the cart has been unhitched and the horse is in the stable. John has been seen on several occasions coming out of the Fort laughing to himself.

The elephant never forgets

When I was a child back in the 1930's, a circus came to Omagh every year. The circus consisted of a ring master, about fifteen horses, twenty dogs, twenty clowns, three elephants, six trapeze artists, four witches, two lions, two tigers, ten monkeys, one snake charmer, two stilt walkers, three tight rope walkers and a magician. They would perform for two weeks in Omagh. When they had finished in Omagh they would pack up their wares and travel to Fintona. They would walk to Fintona with their animals.

Connie Sliven was a very small gentleman. He was a tailor by trade. Connie had a small workshop behind his house along the main Omagh To Fintona road. Connie would sit at the window of his workshop and sew all day from dawn to dusk. While the circus was traveling from Omagh to Fintona, it would pass by Connie house. There was an old woman in the circus by the name of Serann. Everyone was scared of her. She would walk up the road and in her right hand she would carry a big black stick. In the left hand she carried a lead. At the end of the lead there was a Vietnamese potbelly pig. She would wear a pink straw hat on her head with a Rhode-island Red Rooster perched on her hat. She would wag the stick around in the air and shout abuse at anybody she saw. it was believed that she would put a curse on animals and they would die. My mother always said that Serann cursed her turkeys and they all died. An old neighbour, by the name of John Hillock, claimed Serann cursed his cows and they died. So, when people knew when the circus was coming, they would close in all their animals. Behind Serann walked two big jet-black dogs, I couldn't tell what breed. After the two dogs walked three elephants, behind them walked ten or twelve clowns with cart's full of timber. Some horses pulled cages full of tigers, monkeys and lions, last of all came the circus master.

Every year as they approached Connie's house, the convoy would stop. The lead elephant would break from the convoy and go around the back of Connie's tailor shop. When Connie saw the elephant, he would open the window. Then the elephant would put the end of his trunk in through the open window. Connie would go over to the cupboard and pick up a loaf of bread and some peanuts. He would walk back over to his chair and feed the bread and peanuts to the elephant. The elephant would eat the bread and peanuts and then walk back and join the convoy. The convoy would then travel on to Fintona. Every year the same procedure took place, year in and year out and never changed. Until Connie died and another man the name of Mike Rockburn took over the tailor shop and ran the business.

Next year when the circus returns as usual the circus stops in front of Connie's house. The elephant leaves the convoy walks around to the back of the tailor shop. When Mike sees the elephant, he opens the window and the elephant puts his trunk in through the open window. Mike lifts a needle and sticks the needle into the elephant's trunk. The elephant withdraws his trunk from the window and re-joins the circus .The next year when the circus returns, the troupe stops at a farm half a mile down the road from Connie's tailor shop. Three of the elephants break from the convoy, walk into the farmyard, over to the slurry pit and reach their trunks down into the slurry pit and fill their trunks with muck and dirty water. They then return and join the troupe again the troupe moves on towards Fintona until they reach Mike Rockburn's house. The troupe stops. The lead elephant walks around the back of the tailor shop followed by the other two elephants with their trunks full of muck and slurry. Mike opens the window. Instead of one trunk, three trunks enter the building . Mike remembers what he did last year and regrets what he did. The elephants fire the water out from their trunks, and fill the tailor shop with murky, smelly water. Mike and the entire shop and contents were destroyed.

When the elephant's trunks were empty and all the suits and shirts are destroyed, the three elephants walk back and join the rest of the circus troupe. Serann shouts and dances with joy at the elephants destroying the tailor shop. The circus moves on towards Fintona with Serann dancing. The rooster was crowing, the dogs were barking the monkeys were squealing as the lions roared. Nobody ever heard a noise like this noise before. Mike Rockburn spent weeks cleaning up his tailor shop. After five or six weeks, Mike had his tailor shop cleaned up and was back to business as usual.

Until the next year when the circus returned. The three elephants went into the farm yard again and filled their trunks with mucky water. They travelled on to Mike's tailor shop. When the elephants arrived at the back of the tailor shop, Mike refused to open the window. The elephants turned and walked around to the front of the tailor shop reached their trunks in through the open door and blew the dirty water all over Mike and his tailor shop. Mike sold up shop and moved away somewhere else.

The Hearse

Back in the 1980s I was a young fella. I did not like work. I could always mooch all the money I needed from my mother and father. They were always saying 'go out and get yourself a job! We're not made of money!' I got myself several jobs, but I did not like them, so after a short period of time I would give them up. My mother and father were very good. They would give me the last penny in their pocket. One day my mother asked me for the loan of five pounds. On this day the only money I had in the whole world was two pounds. As it was the first time my mother had ever asked me for money, I asked her what she wanted the money for. She said 'your father has not been well this last two weeks and he wasn't working, so there were no wages and the rent is due and there's not a penny in the house'. Those words cut me to the bone. I had learnt a hard lesson about how selfish I had been. Lying about, doing nothing while daddy was working to keep me while he was sick. So I swore to myself that my mother would never have to ask me for money again.

I immediately went out and got myself a job in a local car recycling yard. Nothing spectacular happens. The cars come in, they are weighed and the customer is paid. The car is then lifted by forklift and brought to what is called the detoxing shed. There all the oil, petrol, antifreeze, brake fluid and gear oil is removed. Then the wheels, engine, gearbox, back end and upholstery are removed. The cars are then carried to the bailer where they are bailed and then the bails are stacked for shipment. At the start of every month, a large number of cars would come in due to the number of new cars being bought. I would carry the cars from the weighbridge yard to the detox shed. When detoxed I would then carry them to the bailer where they are bailed up for export. I loved the job and the money was good and I could afford to pay my way at home.

Nothing exceptional happened there very often, until one lovely summer's day at the beginning of June 1991. It had been a very busy week. At about eleven o'clock a man arrived in with an old hearse. He drove the hearse across the weighbridge, collected his money and went on his way. There was nothing unusual about this, as we had taken in hearses before. We had recycled almost every type of vehicle at some time. We had recycled lorries, buses, ambulances, motorcycles, push bikes, wheelchairs wheel barrows. All types of metals. I had been working in the yard just over two years by now. I was good at my job and had been promoted to driving the forklift and the lorry. I drove over with my forklift and picked up the hearse. Just as I lifted the hearse, I froze. There was a man sitting in the back of the hearse. I set the hearse down, got out of the forklift and opened the hearse door. I searched the hearse but could see no one. I climbed back into the forklift again and lifted the hearse. As there was no room in the detox yard, I carried the hearse across the weighbridge yard and set it down close to the main gate. As I set the hearse down, I could see the man sitting in the back of the hearse. I searched the hearse again and could find no one. I reported to the office that I had seen a ghost in the hearse.

The boss was in the office. He laughed and said 'if there is a ghost about the yard I would have him out working!' Everyone in the office laughed, and I felt so stupid for saying what I had seen. As I stood there the boss said 'it is time to start tidying up, since it's a Friday and we don't want to be late finishing. We will deal with it on Monday morning'. I left the office, locked up my fork lift and went to the canteen. I picked up my lunch bag and left for home. When everyone had left for home John Greg locked up the yard as usual.

On Monday morning when John opened the yard gate, he got the shock of his life. The hearse was sitting with its engine running. When I arrived about five minutes later, John and some other workers were standing by the hearse with its engine running. When they told me that the engine was running when they arrived I laughed. John said that when he was locking up on Friday evening he thought he saw a man sitting in the hearse. He then went over and checked and could see no one. I walked over and switched off the engine. As soon as I turned my back the engine started up again. I switched off the engine a second time. This time it did not start up again. I started work as usual. After a short period of time, I started up the forklift and picked up the hearse. I carried it over to the detox yard and left it there. The detox men removed the battery, anti-freeze, petrol, engine oil, gear oil then the engine wheels and upholstery.

When I arrived for work the next morning, nobody could believe what they were seeing or hearing. There was the hearse with the engine sitting beside it running. Our boss arrived on the scene. On hearing what was going on he went over and switched off the engine. In the process he twisted his hand and broke three fingers. I felt like saying to him 'you're not going to get that ghost to work for you!' I did not say what I was thinking because by now it had become too serious. The boss had to go to casualty.

When he arrived back from casualty he said to me pick up the hearse body and engine and throw it all into the bailer. As soon as I approached the hearse the forklift stopped and refused to start. The mechanic worked all day on the forklift and could not get it started. The boss said 'bring over the digger and fill up the bailer'. I started up the digger, lifted two cars and dropped them into the bailer. Then as I went to pick up the hearse the digger stopped and refused to start. By this time it was finishing time so all was left until next morning. When we arrived in for work next morning there was the hearse sitting, engine running. No petrol, no oil. The engine had moved about 30 to 40 meters. The boss arrived and on being informed that nobody would go near the hearse or the engine, the boss said 'that vehicle must go!'

The boss told us to bring it back to the detox yard and put her back together again. Then we were to load it onto the lorry and take it to the scrapyard in Belfast. At that moment the engine stopped. The mechanic got the forklift started. I picked up the hearse and engine and carried them back to the detox yard where the men put the hearse back together. When they were finished they wanted the hearse out of the yard as soon as possible. I picked up the hearse and set it on to the lorry to go to Belfast next morning. When I had it strapped down I put on two extra tying straps. Next morning when we arrived for work the tying straps were all broke the hearse was sitting on the ground beside the lorry with the engine running. When the boss arrived I never saw him in as bad a humour in my life. He switched off the engine. He then walked over to the digger, started up the digger, drove over to the hearse and started to beat the hearse with the digger until he beat the hearse down flat. Then he picked up the hearse and loaded the hearse onto the lorry. He then brought over a Ford Escort, beat it down flat and set it on top of the hearse. He then said 'tie them down now and take them to Belfast'. I said 'I will tie them down, but I am not taking that to Belfast'. He told me to get ready and he would go with me. Myself and another employee named John started to tie down the hearse and escort. Just as I was tightening the second strap, John started to shout and ran across the yard and into the office. I went over to the office to ask John what had happened. When I entered the office, John was sitting crying and his face was as white as a sheet. He was very upset, and the office staff were trying to calm him down. I asked what was wrong with John and was informed that when John was tying down a tying strap he saw a man's head in the hearse. John was so scarred he had to be left home. I finished tying the straps.   About half an hour later our boss arrived back, checked the load and said to put on an extra strap. We tied on two extra straps.

He started up the lorry. The boss and myself headed for Belfast. Everything went well until we hit the M1 motorway. Every now and then the lorry would start to shake. It was like an aeroplane hitting air pockets. It was very scary. About 20 miles up the motorway, the boss shouts to look behind us. I looked round to see the Ford Escort twenty feet up in the air, followed by the hearse. I watched as they both flew over a bridge and down into the river. We travelled to the next slip road and turned for home. We arrived home and everything returned to normal. Sometime later I met the undertaker who owned the hearse. He told me he had not used the hearse for about ten years before he brought it to us. He buried a man who was known to be a bad man and from that very day he could not use the hearse. Every time he went to use the hearse the man was sitting in the back. He said 'I will swear that last week I was going to the airport and I saw the hearse parked on the motorway hard shoulder'. I have been told that the police often receive reports of a suspicious hearse parked on the hard shoulder of the motorway, but they never find it. Every time I travel the M1 motorway I see the hearse parked on the hard shoulder. If you ever travel that way, watch out and you might see a black Rolls Royce hearse with a man sitting in the back.

The house with no chimney

James Clarke married Annie Johnston. James inherited a small farm while
Annie inherited a confectionary shop in town. James ran the farm while
Annie ran the confectionary shop. They lived a good life. They gave birth
to four sons and two daughters. They named their sons John Arthur
George and William their daughters were named Alice and Rebecca. Their
youngest son William was born with only one leg and was special to James
and Annie. They were a very proud couple and reared their family well
John grew up and joined the church. John went on to become a bishop.
Alice and Rebecca married and lived local and reared families. George
married and had two sons. William met a nice neighbour girl by the name
of Sara and fell in love with her and proposed marriage to her. She
accepted, and that's when the trouble started. William had built himself a
nice new house. Arthur, George and their sisters did not approve of
Williams girlfriend because they believed she was below them. Two weeks
before Williams wedding George and Arthur knocked down Williams
house. The feud got so bad Annie wrote to the bishop and asked him to
come home and try and settle the feud.

The bishop came home and stayed for two weeks but could not settle the
feud. Before he left he put a curse on the family and said the day would
come when there would not be a Clarke left in the town. William, the
coward that he was, backed down and never married. Things cooled
down. John still felt bitter but said nothing. Arthur never married and
lived at home with William and his mother and father and ran the farm.
William helped his mother run the confectionary shop. James died and
everyone carried on as normal. Then Annie died. Her death was followed
a short time later by the death of William. One year later Arthur died. By
this time George was suffering from Alzheimer's.

The town had grown around the farm with had made it very valuable.
Annie in her will had left the shop to William. William had made a will
and left his ex-girlfriend Sara everything he owned. By now she had
married and had a Family. Sara's family sold the confectionary shop for a
substantial sum. When it came to the farm William's nieces and nephews
claimed ownership because Arthur had made no will.

The nine nieces and nephews all clamed owner ship of the land the farm had by now been designated as development land. The farm was valued in the region eight to twelve million pounds. Due to the dispute the case had to go to the courts to be settled. It went to the highest court in the land. The courts decided that the farm would be sold and Sara would get William's share which was half and the other half would be divided among the nine nieces and nephews. The court ruled that because the nieces and nephews brought the case they were liable to pay the court costs. When solicitors and courts were paid the nieces and nephews had very little money to get. So, the farm was cursed again.

A developer bought the land and started to build houses on it. When he had only four houses built, the recession came and he could not sell the houses. He went bankrupt, losing everything he owned and owing the banks a lot of money. He also cursed the farm and rued the day he had anything to do with it. The banks now own the farm and the four houses have fallen. The banks have tried on several occasions to sell the farm but could not find a customer.

Today there is not one person by the name of Clarke living in the town.

The School House

The day I met Mr Tcow and his sister Connie Rose, was a lovely Tuesday morning in the middle of July. I was in the office doing some office work. My office is situated at the back of our house and the office door is about four meters from our kitchen door. At about ten o'clock I rose from my desk to get a folder. I looked out of the office window. I could see my wife working in the garden. The garden looked beautiful. The grass had just been mowed the day before. The dahlias were in full bloom, the gladiola were just starting to bloom and the orange marigolds were shinning like the sun The blue lobelia with the white asylum along the border was out of this world. Instead of getting the folder, I went to the kitchen made two cups of tea. I picked up a packet of biscuits and took them outside and sat down at the picnic table joined by my wife. We drank the tea and talked for a while. We rose from the table and walked around the garden, admiring the different flowers. The scent from the roses was just out of this world.

It was so nice; I just did not want to go back to work. I felt as if I was the happiest man in the world.
So, I said to my wife, "I am not going back to work today, will you come with me to Bundoran for the evening?" Bundoran is a nice seaside town, forty miles up the road. My wife replied, "I would love to go, but I am sorry I cannot go because I have a hairdressers appointment today". So instead I decided I would go down to see a man in Drumquin on some business. I informed my wife of my intentions and went to the office to fetch the keys for the van and headed for Drumquin. The direct route from our house to Drumquin is straight over the mountain known as the Pidgeon top. I would never use that road usually because it is too narrow and crooked. I would always travel down to Omagh and then take the main road from Omagh to Drumquin.

The radio in the van was switched on and the eleven o'clock news headlines were just finishing. I switched the radio off, because the sound of it was spoiling the atmosphere of a nice day. I drove down the Letfern Road towards the cross roads, where the Letfern road crosses the Tattyreagh road. A right turn at the cross roads would bring me to Omagh, straight on would bring me over the Pidgeon top. It was so nice today I decided I would go over the Pidgeon top. The Pidgeon top is a mountaintop part of The Sperrin Range. I travelled along uphill and downhill, around one corner after another until I arrived at Tattysallagh school. I turned left past the school. About thirty metres past the school, I saw a man standing holding onto the school sign post. He looked about seventy years of age and looked unwell. He wore a brown felt hat, a long black overcoat and a pair of wellington boots. I stopped the van reversed back. I opened the window and said to him, "are you all right?" He said, "I just took a weak turn". I then opened the van door got out and said to him, "what's your name and where do you live?" He said, "my name is Tomas Tcow and I live in that house down there".

I linked him around to the passenger door of the van got him comfortable in the passenger seat. We drove one hundred meters down the road to two big sandstone pillars with a pair of white gates. The gates were open, so I drove through the open gates and down a short drive way into a farm yard with a large two storey farm house to my left. To my right stood a large two storey stone barn with a Bangor blue slate roof. In front of me was a shed with an open front. I could see the front of an old grey tractor inside the open shed. Directly in front of the tractor stood an old man wearing a long coat and a straw hat. Beside the door there was a green monkey tail pump. Further down from the pump stood two black bicycles against the wall of the house. Over to the front of the barn sat an old grey Morris Oxford car. The yard was spick and span with nothing out of place. The house looked in very good repair and had just been newly painted white. I parked the van with the passenger door as close as possible to the door of the house.

As I got out of the van, a woman who looked about sixty years of age opened the house door. I walked round the back of the van to the passenger door. I opened the door, got the man out of the van and linked him in through the door of the house. We went through the kitchen into a living room. The living room had a lovely brown leather tree piece suite. Underneath the living room window, stood a table covered with a red cloth. There was a white marble fireplace with a turf fire burning. Between the fire and the brown settee sat a glass coffee table. On the table lay a newspaper and a packet of cigarettes. I noticed the house felt very cold for such a nice day, especially with a fire burning. I sat the man down in an armchair in front of the fire. I made him comfortable and left the way I came in. The woman was still standing holding the door. I stopped with her and told her to get the man a doctor. As I left the house, the woman closed the door behind me. The old man was still standing in front of the tractor and had never moved. I got back into the van, started it up and drove towards the gates. The gates were now closed. I got out of the van, walked over to the gates and opened them, got back into the van and drove out onto the road. I could not understand how the gates had been closed. It was only then that I thought about how the woman had never came into the sitting room to check on the man and that she had never spoke to me. As for the man himself, he had never spoke except for when he told me his name and where he lived. I drove on to my destination, parked my van and went into the office and met James McDowell and sorted out my business with him.

When our business was concluded, we came out into the sectary's office. She was making coffee and she asked us would we like to join her in a cup of coffee. I said, "I would love to". Myself, James and the secretary sat down to a nice cup of coffee and a biscuit that I was well ready for. During conversation I told them about the sick man I came across on my way. James' secretary Bethany says "I knew them people. That's Tomas Tcow and his sister Connie Rose Tcow. The old man with the tractor is their father William Tcow". She started to laugh and said, "those people are dead twenty years ago!" I said, "they're not dead because I saw them today". She laughed again and says, "if they're not dead we did a very bad job, because we buried them over twenty years ago". James laughed and all I could do was laugh too. She said, "you're not the first to see them since they died".

I left the office, got into my van and started for home. As I drove up the Glen Road I decided I would go up the mountain for a walk. As I arrived in the townland of Cornashesk, I drove into a farmyard which I knew well and parked my van. Molly the farmer's wife came around the corner of the barn, leading a ram. We exchanged some pleasantries about the ram, the weather and my plan for a walk. I left her, opened the gate and headed up the mountain. Half an hour later I was about half way up the mountain. I stopped for a rest and normally at this point I would always turn back. I stood and looked around. I looked down over the Glen. The scenery was breath taking. All the different colours of the land, the wild flowers and trees. I stood and counted the forty shades of green. For a change I decided I would walk on, to the top of the mountain, which I had never done before.

So, I set off walking again and forty minutes later I arrived at the summit. Looking down I could see Lough Erne and the River Erne in the distance. The mountain was lined with stone walls and dotted with hundreds of sheep. Beauty I have never seen the likes of. I wished I was an artist and could paint what I was seeing and keep it for ever. As I turned to my left, I looked down over the valley and a big white cross appeared in front of me, standing up on the side of the mountain. I kept staring at the cross, wondering what it meant or where it came from. I started thinking about Mr Tcow and a shiver ran down my back. All of a sudden, I felt so cold. I could picture Mr Tcow and his long overcoat by the turf fire. I became scared and started back down the mountain as fast as I could walk, watching the cross as I walked. Then I realised that it looked as if the cross was moving.

After about fifty or sixty yards, the cross started to disappear behind a mound. I kept thinking about what Mr Clarke said about Mr Tcow. I made my way back to the farmyard. As I arrived back in the farmyard, my head was in turmoil. I could barely walk or think straight. I stood by the side of my van and wondered what was wrong with me. Until Packie James Kate the farmer came out of the house and invited me in to join him in a cup of tea. As I entered the kitchen, Mollie pulled out a chair and said, "sit down". I took the chair and sat down across the table from Packie James Kate, who was talking, but to this day I do not know what he was saying.

Mollie came over and set a plate of homemade bread and butter on the table and left again, only to arrive back with two big mugs of tea. She said, "do you take sugar?" I did not answer. She put her hand on my shoulder and gave me a shake and repeated herself, "do you take sugar?" I said "no thank you". Then Packie James Kate says, "are you alright?" At this stage I was starting to regain my composure, and I told my story about Mr Tcow and the cross. Molly says, "I never heard a story like that before. There are no dead men or crosses walking about this country". "Molly," says Packie, "don't be doing that, tell him the truth".

Packie laughed and said, "we have heard about Mr. Tcow, his sister and the old boy running about. Those Tcow's were a very bad bunch when they were alive, they were all highway men and robbed and thieved all they could get their hands on. Thomas Connie Rose and their father William would go down to Donegal and block the Glenshane pass and rob everyone who came along the road. As for the cross, it is real. The cross stands in a field that field belonged to a family who were evicted from their house and farm by a bank. One son went to London and did well for himself and some years later he came home. He bought the field back and paid three thousand pounds to have that cross erected in the field". Packie stood up and said, "come with me." We went out, got into Packie's car and drove up the Glen Road about one mile. He parked the car and we got out and walked up a lane to the field. There stood a big white cross standing about fifteen feet tall. We examined the cross, said a prayer and headed back to Packie's house. Some of the stories Packie James Kate told me I dare not repeat. I then said my good byes and headed for home. I decided I would go back home over the mountain again.

As I had sorted the mystery of the moving cross, I would sort out the mystery of Mr Tcow. On arriving back at Mr Tcow's house, I stopped the van and got out. I stood on the road and looked at the house and yard. I could not believe what I was seeing. The big two storey house looked derelict. The farmyard was overgrown with weeds. The nice big white gates were all brown and rusted. The tractor had gone and the roof of the open shed had collapsed in on itself. The stone walls of the barn stood derelict. The slate roof had gone. I stood there in amazement, until a woman came up the road with a little dog on a lead and startled me. I said to her, "who lives here?" She says, "nobody lives there now, an old brother and sister used to live there by the name of Tcow, but they're dead years ago. People talk of seeing Mr Tcow walk up and down the farmyard". I left the gates not knowing what to say or think. I walked over and got into the driver's seat of my van and closed the door. As I clicked my seat belt there was Mr Tcow sitting in the passenger seat of the van beside me. I started up my van and raced up the road as fast as the van would go. As I approached the signpost there was smoke rising from the signpost like the chimney of a house. As I passed the school signpost Mr Tcow disappeared. I drove the rest of the road home scared and puzzled. That was nearly fifteen years ago. To this day I have heard different people tell stories about seeing Mr Tcow and their experiences of him not being good. I have not travelled that road since.

The Top hat

It was a lovely autumn evening in the year of 1950, when my older brother says "will you come with me, I am going up to Barney Mc Connell's to get my bicycle fixed". I said I would, because I loved a ride on a bicycle. He gets his bicycle and puts me up on the bar, and we were off, him cycling and me sitting on the bar. As we travelled along the road it was lovely - my brother cycling and telling me stories. Everything went well until we arrived at the bicycle repair shop. Barney examines the bicycle and says "you will have to leave it with me as I am very busy, I will have no time to fix it until tomorrow afternoon". My brother says "that's all right, I will come back and collect it tomorrow evening" and we left to walk the two miles home. By this time it was dark. We walked along the road talking ninety till a dozen. We arrived at the back gate of Colonel McClintock's big house, known as McCourt's corner. As we turned the corner, there in the middle of the road stood a very small man with a stick in his left hand. His hands were as big as a number 7 shovel. He had a nose as bent as a cutter of a plough. He wore a long black coat and a tall hat. When we went to pass him, he stood in the middle of the road and would wag his stick. As we moved to the left side of the road he would move to the left and stand in front of us and wag his stick. We then moved to the right hand side of the road he would stand in front of us and wave his stick. No matter what we tried, he stood in front of us waving his stick and would not let us pass. My brother says to me "we will go back". We turned back and walked back up the road about fifty or sixty yards and talked about what we would do to get home. My brother says "we will beat him up; we will be well fit as there are two of us and he is an old man". I agreed and we armed ourselves with two ash sticks out of the hedge and down the road again, me praying that when we got back the small man would be gone. As we rounded McCourts corner, there he was standing in the middle of the road. As we tried to pass, he stood in front of us waving his stick. No way were we going to get past. My brother swung his stick, hitting the man's hat. The hat flew across the road and landed on top of the hedge. The wee man ran across the road to pick up his hat and we ran past. We ran to the top of the hill and stopped for a rest. When I looked back the wee man was trying to get his hat of the hedge with his bald head shinning like a second moon and him scolding to himself. We walked on home and left him to get on with retrieving his hat. When we arrived home and told daddy about the man, he told us the man was a ghost and at certain times at night nobody got past him and that we were very lucky to get past.

The turf

Charlie Wilkinson lived on his own on top of Morley Mountain between Fintona and Omagh. Charlie made a living by rearing sheep and cutting turf. Charlie seldom came down from the mountain. Once every year, Charlie came down to Fintona mart to sell his sheep. It was the year of 1999 in the month of September that Charlie came down to Fintona to sell his sheep. By this time Charlie was heading for fifty years of age and was reassessing his life. On arriving at Fintona mart he met Joe Doak. Joe and Charlie had been friends for years. Joe and Charlie decided they would go to the pub for a drink.

When in the pub, Charlie told Joe he wanted to get married and was looking for a woman. Joe told him to go down to Tattyreagh and see a man by the name of Red McFee, as McFee was a good match maker. One year later Joe and Charlie meet up again at the sheep sales and went for a drink. Joe asked Charlie if he ever did get a woman. Charlie says "no, I have changed my mind. I don't want a woman now". Joe asks what had changed his mind. Charlie says, "I went down to Tattyreagh and met Red McFee and McFee says if you don't hurry up and get a woman you will be too late". McFee says, "I will get you a woman". He says, "there's a pub in Omagh by the name of Cissy Janes. You be there on Saturday night and I will meet you and introduce you to a good woman".

Charlie told Joe"I went down to Cissy Janes, met McFee and he introduced me to this nice looking woman. She was wearing a fur coat and her name was Agnes. Mc Fee says, this is a good woman for you, yes? I said, she looks nice, but tell me, what's good about her? He says, she is the best darts thrower in town. I says to Agnes, would you like a drink? She says, yes, I will have a wee brandy and port. I take Agnes by the hand and we walk up to the bar and I order a brandy and port for Agnes and an orange juice for myself and we get talking. While you would blink an eye, Agnes was ready for another brandy and port and another and another. In no time I had bought her six brandy and ports. She then stands up and takes her coat off and says it is very warm in here, and I says to her, it's no wonder you are warm. You have the price of twenty bags of my turf in you! I left at that and went home and decided to forget about looking for a woman".

THE TWO BROTHERS

There were two brothers by the by the names of John and Mick McGregg. John and Mick lived with their mother Maggie. Maggie was a very religious woman with strong beliefs which she tried to instil into her sons. Their father had died when they were very young. Maggie with her sons owned and farmed a farm of good land in the townland of Tattyreagh. John and Mick could never agree on anything, they argued and fought all the time with their mother Maggie caught in between them. Maggie would always get cross with them and say, "If you don't stop now, I will call Doctor McGinn". Doctor McGinn was the parish priest and they would always settle down because Doctor McGinn was known as a good man with great powers for curing the sick. This carried on and on until Doctor McGinn died and six months latter Maggie died. Then the fighting started about who owned the land, as well as that the two men started drinking heavily.

One Saturday night, Mick was coming home from the pub full drunk when it started to rain very heavy. Mick went and stood in close to the chapel door for shelter. As he stood close to the door the door opened. Mick went inside and sat down and fell asleep. When Mick woke in the middle of the night, to his surprise all the lights in the church were lit. Dr McGinn was standing on the altar dressed in full vestments looking down at him. Mick ran out of the church and never stopped running until he got home. All the next week Mick never spoke to John or anyone else and kept thinking about Doctor McGinn. On the following Saturday night, the same thing happened to John on his way home from the pub. John came home and never spoke until Wednesday morning. When Mick says to him, "what's wrong with you, you have not spoken in four days, and I have never seen you work so hard?" John tells Mick about falling asleep in the chapel and dreaming about seeing Dr McGinn. Mick says to John, "it wasn't a dream, it was real because I saw him too".

The two men spoke long and hard about their experience, the first sensible conversation since their Mother died. They decided they would go back to the chapel on Saturday night and try and investigate what happened. At about 2 am on Sunday morning the two men arrived at the church door. The door was locked. As they turned to leave, the door opened. The men entered and sat down. As they sat down the lights in the church lit up and Dr McGinn appeared standing on the altar. Mick and John sat there, wondering what was happening. There they were sitting in the church which they had refused to go near for years. John rises and walks up the aisle to the altar. He stands thinking for a while and then says, "Dr McGinn what do you want us for?" The priest says, "your mother asked me to say a mass for you and Mick, and I died before I got to say it. I cannot get into heaven until I say the mass and I want you to serve the mass for me". John and Mick agreed to serve the mass for Dr McGinn. Dr McGinn said the mass immediately.

When the mass was said, Dr McGinn disappeared and Mick and John left for home. As they left the church, the door locked behind them as the lights went out. John and Mick never drank or fought again, and they attended church every week since.